SAVING THE DINOSAURS

Jane Waller was born in Aylesbury, Buckingham-
shire and brought up in Oxfordshire. She has a BA
in Sculpture as well as an MA in Ceramics from
the Royal College of Art. She has written copiously
on subjects as wide ranging as ceramics and
fashion, and her first published children's novel,
Below the Green Pond, was voted among the Pick of
the Year by the Federation of Children's Book
Clubs.

In *Saving the Dinosaurs* she has combined
impeccably researched fact with wild fantasy and
a vibrant imagination. She now lives with her husband in London by the River Thames.

SAVING
THE DINOSAURS

A Death Star Heads for Planet Earth

Jane Waller

A PIPER ORIGINAL
PAN MACMILLAN
CHILDREN'S BOOKS

First published 1994 by Pan Macmillan Children's Books

a division of Pan Macmillan Publishers Limited
Cavaye Place London SW10 9PG
and Basingstoke

Associated companies throughout the world

ISBN 0 330 33098 5

1 3 5 7 9 8 6 4 2

A CIP catalogue record for this book is available from
the British Library

Phototypeset by Intype, London
Printed by Cox & Wyman Ltd, Reading

This book is dedicated to my godchild,
Robert John Waller

ACKNOWLEDGEMENTS

To my husband, Michael Vaughan-Rees, for editing, encouragement and support; to Andy Currant and Ann Lum of the Department of Palaeontology in the Natural History Museum, for their advice; to Gerald Taylor and David Waller for their help and advice; Jan and Phil Truman, Gill Pyrah, Lyn and David Griffin and the Hanna family for their help; and Isabel Barratt, my Editor, and lastly, Michael Allaby and James Lovelock (who are mentioned in the story itself) for technical advice from their book *The Great Extinction*.

PREFACE

Dinosaurs died out 65 million years ago – and long before Man put in an appearance. At the end of the Cretaceous Age, nearly three-quarters of all living species vanished. As far as we know, almost all the dinosaurs disappeared. This mass extinction marks the boundary between two of the great divisions of geological time: the Mesosoic Era and the Tertiary Period.

As far as possible I have endeavoured to be accurate with information, and readers may be startled by the number of birds, animals and flowering trees which were already in existence by the late Cretaceous Age. However, my "horse creature" would have been a *very* early type of *Eohipus*. As far as we know, *Eohipus*, which was only 30 cm high, evolved a little later. The *Brontosaurus* – or *Apatosaurus* – had died out before the end of the Cretaceous Age; however, our dinosaurs in this story, *Opisthocoelicaudia*, were one type of large sauropod to survive until the time of the great extinction. They resemble the *Camarasurus*, but their tails are held out straight and their shoulders are higher.

The continents occupied more or less the same latitudinal positions in the Cretaceous Age that they occupy today; their drift was mainly east and west. Early in the period there was more dry land than in late Cretaceous times when, little by little, the seas encroached, so that the total land area was reduced. The Wookey Hole area may have been under water, though I have allowed the top of it to appear above.

CONTENTS

Chapter One

THE BIRTHDAY PRESENT

When the parcel arrived it was strangely heavy and completely covered with stamps.

"It looks as if it's been round the world three times instead of just coming from America," said Peter. He had to sign for the parcel before it was even allowed into the house.

"Can I open it now?"

Mrs Phillips looked at her son's face. A mop of floppy hair covered one brown eye so the other had to do all the pleading. Although it wasn't his birthday for three weeks, she knew Peter had saved hard for this new computer disc. She could hardly expect him to wait.

"OK, go on then." She nodded, then put on her gardening gloves, gathered her basket – full of trowels, twine and a pruning knife – and went into the garden to plant her new packet of cabbage seeds. She was so pregnant, she waddled like a duck.

Clutching the parcel, Peter raced to his room. This was the new disc he'd chosen from his friend Ivan's computer manual; the very latest thing – a disc in 3D called "Journey into Space". "I'm probably the first person in England to receive one of these," he thought.

Peter's computer had a curved screen and a digital clock set into its base. He knew that his father had bought him this expensive American model because he was away in Bangkok for nine long months. "All the same, I wish he could be home for my birthday; but I suppose he can't." And Peter could hardly grumble; if it wasn't for the birthday money his father had already sent, he wouldn't have saved enough for the disc.

He soon found out why the parcel was so heavy. It contained a flat, square packet, and a lumpy thing that must be some kind of manual. He opened the flat packet, and there it was – sealed in fine cellophane and protected in a plastic case. Quickly he opened it. But as he pulled out the disc, he noticed a strong chemical smell and, for an instant, the disc felt sticky. As this dried, he saw that his fingerprints had been trapped, sealed into the surface for ever. "How peculiar," he thought.

The grooves – or rather tracks – on the new disc were so dense they shimmered in rainbow prisms. Peter beamed the disc round his room, amazed at the startling rays that bounced off the walls. He glinted some on to the photo of himself and Ivan on their mountain bikes. Then he flashed some over the dinosaur chart they'd made at school, colouring his carefully drawn brachiosaurus and stegosaurus in streaks of yellow and mauve. "I've never seen anything like this before; it must be a new type, just invented."

Eagerly he switched on the computer, slotted in the disc, then closed his curtains to darken the room. Now at last he could try out his special helmet with eyepieces and earphones which he had already bought. The screen curved around him, glowing into readiness as he settled himself. The machine was purring through various stages when an order appeared, asking him to type in his name and address. He'd never had to do that before. Impatiently he obeyed: Peter Phillips, 3A Richmond Row, London . . . This seemed to satisfy it, for immediately up came the title "Journey into Space". And it really *was* 3D. This is going to be good, very good. He leaned forward, absorbed.

The sound effects were so real that Peter almost felt himself rising from the ground. He had to grip his chair. Soon he was gaining speed rapidly, sliding through cloud-layer after cloud-layer, their wisps curling past his face, then trailing off to the side. This was terrific – better than he'd ever imagined. Now he was above Earth's atmosphere, ejected into space. Stars and planets spun across the screen, some seeming to come from behind him, while great clouds of interstellar gas loomed ahead. A moon rolled up from below, huge, and scarred with craters. This curved away and . . . Wow! He'd left it way behind and was travelling faster. They nearly crashed into an asteroid belt which hurtled by. He could see their craggy surfaces as clearly as if—

Then suddenly the screen shook. Planets, moons and asteroids melted, softening like noodles as they slipped out of control towards him. They fell in a meteor shower of flattened discs down the front of the screen, disappearing, it felt, almost in his lap.

"No! No! Stop!" This must be some kind of computer virus!

But he could do nothing; his program was ruined.

For a moment or two Peter sat in silence. What a birthday gift! And he'd saved for this disc for so long.

3

Then Peter – normally easy-going and content – grew really angry. Why should *his* program be wrecked? He'd heard about such viruses, but what a mean trick. One after another he pushed the keys. Nothing happened. Then he pressed ENTER. The screen changed. A message appeared in bold type:

DEPARTMENT OF DEFENSE. OFFICIAL. TOP SECRET.
FOR THE ATTENTION OF PETER PHILLIPS,
3A Richmond Row,
London,
Ontario.

"London, Ontario? That's in Canada. But the rest of my address is correct ... except they forgot the post code."

From the date in the corner it seemed to have been written only a week ago. He pressed ENTER again.

Operation Time Loop, it stated: Series One. Experiment One.

On the left of the screen were places from all over the world; on the right, various ages in history to which you could travel. Curious, Peter ran his eye down the list. From London, England, he noticed, you could travel back to the time of the ancient Pharaohs, or back as far as the Cretaceous Age. The Cretaceous Age! That's what they were studying at school, the Jurassic and Cretaceous Ages – the time when dinosaurs were around.

SELECT AND ENTER ordered the program.

He selected The Cretaceous Age. Now the screen changed. There was a graph, plotted in great detail, from

4

which dipped three carefully drawn loops. At the base of each was a launching place and date. The first was: The Dinosaur Gallery in the Natural History Museum. April 5th. The second: The Palm House in Kew Gardens. April 15th. The third: Wookey Hole in Somerset. April 25th.

It was a coincidence really that the first launch was from the Natural History Museum. That was where their end-of-term class excursion was going – and on the same date! "Very strange!" thought Peter. "Almost as if it was meant to happen."

Then Peter realized that, slowly and cleverly, he was being drawn into a different game. Although he was fond of dinosaurs, this was not the program he'd ordered. "The one I selected from Ivan's catalogue was definitely 'Journey into Space', and that's what I want. I suppose I'd better go to Ivan's and check the ad. Maybe there's something I didn't read."

Peter wrenched off his helmet, strode across the room, ripped open the curtains and threw up the window. Out in the garden, his mother had raked a long furrow, a rich, fine brown streak across the earth, and was hovering above it, trying to bend over her great pod stomach to sow the cabbage seeds.

"Mum!" he shouted.

She looked up, red-faced with effort, her silly straw gardening hat flopped over her face. "What is it?"

"I'm just cycling over to Ivan's."

"OK, dear. Don't be late for lunch."

As Peter put his new disc back in its plastic case, the rainbow rays glanced into his eyes and stung them so that several tears trickled down. Now he would have to send it back to America, then wait for ages for a proper disc to arrive.

Peter crammed his baseball cap on his head. He always wore this whenever he went out. It had been sent from Bangkok for Christmas, together with a cheque to get a mountain bike. Outside his bedroom, Peter banged into a playpen stacked against the wall. Baby things were getting everywhere, waiting to be moved into *his* room. That was another thing going wrong. Because his room was large, it was "just right for baby". It would house the playpen on the landing, the cot which blocked the hall, and the new pram. Peter refused to move until the baby actually arrived, because he was to go into the small room, his father's old study. He was not looking forward to that. He would virtually have to sit on the end of his bed to work his computer. Peter smiled at his computer before closing the door. He realized, guiltily, that it was probably the most important thing in his life at the moment – and it wasn't even a person! In the kitchen, he tipped his school books on to the table and stuffed the parcel inside his satchel.

Out in the garden, Mrs Phillips paused in her sowing to watch her son cycle past the hedge. She was pleased to see him out; he *should* be out on a warm day like this, not cooped up in a dark room with a computer. She worried that since his father went he was spending more and more time with that dratted machine. "It isn't good for him. That nice, open, friendly face shouldn't be spoiled with bags under the eyes. And that hair ... I must really cut it. Oh dear! There's so much to think about. How *am* I going to cope? I didn't even check he'd done his homework." Mrs Phillips crunched the empty seed packet in her hand. "Bye," she yelled as the figure disappeared.

"Bye," Peter called. He needn't have bothered telling her he was going; she seldom noticed him nowadays. Her obsession with the baby didn't involve him, and he felt shut out. Before, when Mum was only obsessed with the garden, she had shared her love of flowers and trees with him, teaching him many of their names. Now everything centred round the baby. "A gift from God, coming ten years after you, Peter. It's a miracle. You'll love your baby brother, darling, you'll see – I'm certain it'll be a boy."

Peter didn't want to. He knew just what to expect: Ivan's mother had just had another baby, only there weren't ten years in between – she was always having them. Ivan warned him that it meant crying in the night, sick and dribble over everything, baby smells and nappies. Peter knew that, with his father away, he would have to help look after him most of the time.

He pedalled faster, letting the wind race past his face and was soon at Ivan's. He went in the back way, and straight to Ivan's room. Today he took in its size, realizing it was even bigger than the one he was to give up at home. Ivan had his own key so he could lock himself in to escape from the rest of his family – his mother and sisters would keep bursting in with snacks. His father, a successful lawyer, doted on his eldest son, aware that he was exceptionally bright, though sometimes excited and difficult. That boy Peter was a good influence on Ivan. He was level-headed and sensible – though not, of course, as intelligent as his own son. So Mr Topolski bought Ivan the same mountain bike as Peter's, and got him the same computer for his room so they could swap discs. He was pleased Ivan had found himself a friend so fast, since they had moved only recently into the district. Mr Topolski was responsible, too, for the pile of the latest computer manuals and magazines in the corner of the room. It was from one of these that Peter had selected his new disc.

Ivan Topolski was at his computer when Peter burst in.

"Hi. What's the trouble? You look positively livid." He laughed at Peter's baseball cap, put on askew so his mop of hair nearly covered his nose; then he saw the parcel Peter took from the satchel. "Hey, is that your new disc? Give it here. Let's have a go."

But Peter was already searching the magazines to find the one that advertised the disc.

"Here it is, the ad. See! It definitely offers 'Journey into Space' – it doesn't mention any other program. It's got to be some kind of mistake."

Peter unwrapped the disc and handed it to Ivan. He, too, was startled by its brightness. It glinted briefly on his spectacles, forcing his eyes to close.

"Phew! What have we here? It's incredibly tough and shiny." Eagerly he fed it into his computer, which buzzed away, loading the disc. The promised title "Journey into Space" appeared, then immediately stopped to demand the user's address. As Peter obeyed, it went straight into the Top Secret message.

"Wow! I see what you mean; this 'Journey into Space' must be a cover-up for the *real* program – one meant to be sent to a Peter Phillips living in London, Ontario. That's remarkable, don't you see? The addresses are practically identical. Positively a one in a million chance of that happening – or even less. Let's check what's going on."

Ivan, a whizz at maths and physics, had already shot to the top of the class, and they were even thinking of putting him in the one above. Right now he pushed his glasses further on to his nose, a habit that meant concentration.

"This certainly wasn't meant for you, was it? It seems a Mr Witkins sent the disc from a top security lab in Texas to this other scientist, Peter Phillips. It must be a time-travel game."

Ivan read the first page, but was soon frowning. His voice when he next spoke was serious and quiet. "There's something dead odd here. It says that time loops have been discovered, using the Chaos Theory. I've heard about that. And it's certainly top secret – there's a US military number. Look!"

He pushed ENTER, and the time-loop graph appeared. "Wow! It seems you can choose some age in the past and go back to it. Ah, you've chosen one already – The Cretaceous Age. Travelling back 65 million years . . . This is good, man!" Ivan looked up at his school dinosaur chart to check what would be around. "Great!" he exclaimed. "Monster creatures! Tyrannosaurus, triceratops . . . This is going to be smashing!" He pushed at his spectacles and read the following page.

But Peter, sitting next to him, grew mad. Ivan didn't care that his space program had been ruined. "Ivan—"

Ivan shushed him. He had just noticed how the first time loop coincided with their class excursion to the Natural History Museum. "Listen . . . 'All time loop

9

connections are at fourteen thirty hours precisely. The disc is needed in order to travel. Hold in the hand. Be in exactly the right location. Stand upright; feet together' . . ."

Ivan turned to Peter, and he looked strange. "You do realize there's something really weird here. Almost as if . . . as if it isn't a game at all but the real thing . . . That somehow one *could* travel back using these time-loop connections. That, if you stood in the right place at the right time, you could go back thousands – no, millions of years . . . However, on second thoughts . . . No, of course not. What a fat-head! How could you make such a jump without some tremendous source of energy? Even if a time loop *was* incredibly near to a point of entry into another age . . ."

Ivan's face relaxed. "It's all right, Peter, I'm not going loony – really! It *is* only a game. It has to be. You see, it says here that you have to use an activator. You need to have something called a power pack, and there isn't one . . ."

"There was something else that came in the parcel," Peter almost whispered. "Something incredibly heavy. Heavy enough to have taken up all those stamps."

Ivan's face paled as he saw Peter reach inside the parcel for the lumpy thing; and he bent forward to help rip the paper, to reveal a heavy black object. Suddenly afraid to touch it, they stared. It had a plug on one side and on the top of it was printed POWER PACK.

Chapter Two

THE NATURAL HISTORY
MUSEUM

On April 5th, the school coach was crowded. Peter and Ivan sat near the front, feeling tense and excited. Before leaving that morning they had loaded the dinosaur program, matched their watches with the digital clock in the computer – set precisely to Greenwich Mean Time – and, finally, plugged in the Energy Activator Power Pack. Immediately it started to tick softly – like a waiting bomb.

Ivan decided to use his house for the operation because he could lock the door. "We don't want anything silly happening – like your mother switching the computer off – so you couldn't travel back."

"Or turning my room into a nursery – if the baby arrived," added Peter, nervously.

"Yes, you need to watch out for babies. They can arrive any time – and there's panic all round, I know."

Just then Mr Carter, their class teacher, got on and stood beside the driver, facing them. "Now I want you all to reassemble afterwards at three thirty. Our coach will be waiting to pick you up in Exhibition Road. And

11

don't forget, although it's the end-of-term treat, you'll be writing about your visit for our dinosaur project. The best pieces will be read out in class in the final week of term. See you behave. No one's to do anything silly. We don't want to let the school down, do we? And remember, drinks and sandwiches in the basement eating area only. Right then, everyone here?"

Everybody was – except for Miss Rawlings, or Rawley as she was called. She came puffing up, checking her watch as she raced along. There was a lot of clapping as she boarded. Then the engine revved; the excursion had begun.

As the journey progressed, both boys grew rather quiet. Ivan absent-mindedly ate all his sandwiches. "What if time is different back there?' he worried to himself. "Supposing three hours in the Cretaceous Age is the same as three centuries in ours? What if Peter returns and everyone he knows is dead? I'd better not say that aloud."

Peter was feeling scared – and guilty. He knew the disc wasn't meant for him, that he was dabbling in something not his concern. "When I arrive there, just suppose I have an accident? Suppose I get eaten, for example, and never return? How could Ivan explain? 'Ahemmm. Sorry, Mrs Phillips, but your son's disappeared into the Cretaceous Age, somewhere inside the Natural History Museum.'" Ivan had tried to convince him that time travel was possible, but Peter wasn't so sure. How *could* anyone go back physically? It had never been done before – or had it? What happened to all those people who *did* just disappear and were never heard of again? Agitated, Peter fingered the disc-case tucked in his jeans pocket. Maybe he should leave the disc in its case and just *pretend* at the last minute that he had taken it out, pretend it hadn't worked; that it really was just a game after all. Yes! That's what he'd do.

His mind made up, suddenly he felt very relieved. He looked in his sandwich box. His mother had excelled herself for a change: date, walnut and cream cheese sandwiches, a bar of chocolate, an enormous apple and a carton of squash. He would enjoy them once the panic was over. For the rest of the journey he relaxed; even cracked a joke or two. Ivan was impressed. "He's far braver than I imagined, acting so casual."

When the coach arrived, most of the class went down to the sandwich area to eat their lunch, or they got drinks out of the machines. Peter and Ivan found themselves drawn to the new Dinosaur Gallery, where they needed to be at two thirty precisely. Their stomachs tightened as they gazed up at the monsters soaring above: huge creatures, their fossilized bones stapled together with iron clips. They all looked so ancient and mysterious. Some had tiny heads on the end of necks so long and high up you could hardly see where they joined the body.

Suddenly, roaring noises from the modern holograms and movable dinosaurs in the next gallery echoed menacingly in their own, as if they came from inside the tiny heads. Every creature, both in and outside the cases, seemed to be staring at Peter from bony, eyeless sockets.

"What would it really be like to meet a living dinosaur face to face?" Ivan was saying. "No human being has ever seen one before. Remember, Carter taught us that human beings appeared on the earth sixty-two million years *after* the dinosaurs died out. Come to think

13

of it, no dinosaur would ever have seen a human being either. I wonder what they'd think if they did?" Ivan was getting very excited. He turned to Peter and tugged at his sleeve. "Hey, Peter, couldn't I travel back with you? Couldn't we both hold the disc and go together? It's almost time. Please say I can."

Peter looked at Ivan's face. He'd never seen it like this – all soft and pleading, with an engaging smile on his wide mouth. Peter faltered. "I don't know. Let me think . . . I . . ."

"Oh, come on. Let me. Decide! It's almost time."

Ivan didn't ask for things in this way usually: he demanded them, and in such a way you couldn't refuse. For a moment Peter liked the feeling of Ivan wanting something from him. He felt quite flattered in fact.

But it was then he found himself beginning to sweat. He had decided, quite suddenly, that he *would* go through with it after all – not just pretend, but do the thing for real. Yes, but he would also do it alone. He was scared and he could feel his heart beating away, but he had started to feel a great longing to see a pterosaur swooping, a triceratops bellowing. Ivan was right, he would be the only human in the whole world ever to have seen a dinosaur alive . . .

"No, I've decided to go on my own," he said solemnly. "Besides, I need somebody to cover for me while I'm away. We don't know how long I'll be, do we? The scientists probably don't even know that themselves. After all, it is an experiment."

Ivan looked crestfallen, but he knew Peter wouldn't change his mind. And Peter felt mean. "Look, I'll tell you what," he bargained. "You can come with me next

14

time if you want to, on the fifteenth. Anyway, I may not even *see* a dinosaur this first time."

"Well, go on your own then, it's almost time. You know, if you're going to disappear, you really ought to hide behind something."

"I could go over there, behind that big cabinet. The disc flashes, remember, and I need to take it out of its case to hold it in my hand."

"Haven't you got it out ready, you dolt? Ivan panicked. 'You'll miss it altogether if you don't hurry. One second either side of two thirty may be too late. Go on! Move!"

Peter had grown very hot under his yellow jersey, and his legs felt stiff and heavy. When he reached the cabinet, he stumbled, almost dropping the disc. He leaned against the glass to steady himself. It shook noisily. An attendant shot an angry glance their way. He started to walk towards them.

The seconds were ticking towards 2.30 p.m.

"Hurry!" said Ivan, his voice hoarse and broken. "Get behind the cabinet. I'll ask the attendant something, to distract him."

Peter's mouth had gone dry, and he was attempting to stand firmly, with legs slightly apart. The disc, clutched in his hand, glinted. It caught the eye of a little boy with a freckled face and bright ginger hair who was staring through the other side of the cabinet. Startled, he looked up at Peter – but the larger boy suddenly disappeared.

Chapter Three

TRAVELLING BACK

Peter was still standing, the disc clutched in one hand, his sandwich box in the other. His knees trembled so much that he was forced to lean back against the rough base of the fern tree; and there he stayed, eyes tightly shut, until his heart slowed down and his teeth stopped chattering. Once he felt steadier, he opened his eyes and stared.

He found himself in a clearing, very bright where the sun beat down in the centre, and fading at the edges where darkness dappled the trees. The noise was deafening, coming from everywhere at once: chatterings, squeakings, flappings, slidings, scrapings, croakings . . . Right overhead, some strange bird-like things sounded as though they were trying out first editions of their songs in the branches but needed more practice.

Peter tried to stay calm as he returned the disc to its case and tucked it back in his pocket. He looked at his watch: that was working normally, but then it was supposed to be shockproof and waterproof. Next he took off his jersey and sat on it to collect his thoughts. He took some deep breaths and tried to relax. The air here was heavy and hot – cleaner than at home, and full of perfumes; rich sweet smells, absolutely delicious – scented like nothing he knew.

Suddenly Peter smiled. It had worked! Here he was in the Cretaceous Age. It felt very strange and wonderful.

"Perhaps I'd better look around to see where I am," he decided, when he felt recovered. Replacing his baseball cap, in case he got sunburnt, he got up and wandered round the glade. The perfumes seemed to be coming from all kinds of blossoms, especially from some great red, waxy, trumpet-shaped flowers that wrapped around the boughs in ropy vines. He was surprised to find so many flowers about until he remembered that it was in Jurassic times that there were only ferns and palms. Some of the trees smelled strongly from their bark; cinnamon smells, drawn out by the heat. And there were darker, pungent perfumes, reminding him of the inside of his grandmother's oriental wooden chest.

As he brushed past flowers, he disturbed great lumbering insects that droned across the glade with low buzzings: immense bumble bees in bright, stripy colours, flying with their legs dangling down; dragonfly insects with blue and emerald-green iridescent wings. They danced in lacy loops drawn through the light and shade. Nothing seemed to mind him being there; things went about their usual way – and it wasn't frightening at all; it was smashing, quite unbelievably fantastic.

Soon Peter felt too hot. "I'd better drink some of my orange," he thought. He returned to his tree fern and sat under its shade. He was hungry now, so he started on his sandwiches. Overhead the birds had broken into an argument, and Peter wondered if they were a kind of archaeopteryx, the first bird, only not behaving as he knew them – spread out and nicely drawn in a text book – but fighting tooth and claw over the seed-pods. Their beaks were long and sharp, their eyes beady and bright.

"Shut up!" shouted Peter, delighted. Momentarily they stopped squawking to peer down. The seed-cone they were fighting over dropped, narrowly missing his head. Peter picked it up and hid it in his pocket. The birds looked disappointed, then angrily started to squabble over something else. Some furrier creatures, alerted by his shout, ran up the tree-trunk to fling themselves recklessly off, like flying squirrels.

Peter sighed and leaned back, taking in the colours and sounds. This was better than any film or computer game – and it was real ... "Rather like going back to the beginning of everything," he thought. He took out the apple, leaving the chocolate bar for later, then hid the plastic sandwich box under his jersey. The silly cartoon dinosaur on it annoyed him and seemed so stupid here.

It was as he was biting into his apple that he saw the most perfect of things, scenting the air, coming quietly towards him. It was a very primitive creature rather like a horse – a miniature one.

"Oh!" he breathed. "Come on little thing, come on." He bit off a chunk of apple and placed it on his palm, which he made very flat and encouraging. The tiny creature sniffed excitedly, then looked Peter straight in the eye. And it was almost as if he understood. "Is it all right? May I?"

"You've probably never tasted apple before; it probably hasn't even been invented. Come on then."

The horse snuffled its warm nose at the delicacy, then took it gently from the outstretched hand and crunched it eagerly. The rest of the apple was divided between them, but the core he buried in the ground with his penknife. "You never know," he mused, "I might have planted the very first apple tree." That pleased him, and he was about to pat the horse again when a twig cracked sharply at the end of the glade and it galloped away – only not galloped exactly, for Peter had noticed that, instead of hooves, the tiny creature had four neat toes.

The cracking twig noise had been made by the first really large animal Peter had seen: a giant woodlouse, but *really* giant, with wide feelers searching this way and that. The creature's hind legs copied exactly those in front, belting along like the treads of a tank. If there was a boulder in the way, up and over they crawled, rather than take an easier route. Noises from the creature's mouth tumbled out at the same speed as the legs. Peter felt that if he could only concentrate on the cracked, high-pitched voice, he would be able to know what it said. As the woodlouse went past, all the legs screeched to a halt: it had smelled the crumbs.

"Oh, so you're after my sandwich?" Happily Peter fed the prehistoric creature with bread. It seemed very keen on the modern food.

The woodlouse answered his thoughts. "Yes, don't *you* like trying out new things?"

"Of course," Peter replied. Now he ceased to care whether he merely thought the conversation or said it aloud. It seemed that he *did* know what it said; he couldn't think how. Was he understanding from somewhere far inside his brain, by instinct? Or from some way that people no longer used, a kind of telepathy? Perhaps a kind used by ancient man?

This was such an odd thing that Peter looped the

jersey round his waist, picked up his sandwich box, and caught up with the creature as it beetled along. Nor could he resist occasionally touching the woodlouse's back. The shiny segments of carapace slid one against another, rasping and creaking like a newly polished saddle.

At the end of the glade they passed a majestic tree, covered with creamy-red fruits. While the woodlouse snuffled around, Peter picked up a fallen one. It was squashy and ripe with raised lumps on the outside. He was about to cut it open with his knife when he felt woodlouse feelers brush against his leg, and the mouth-part make a light, vertical scraping.

"You can eat that fruit if you like, if you're still hungry. Your skin tells me you won't be poisoned."

Peter was astonished. Again, he understood. He ate the pinkish pulp, and it was good – very thirst-quenching. So he took two more to eat while he walked, because the creature would not delay.

Soon Peter found that, if he didn't concentrate so hard but sort of relaxed his mind, he could understand perfectly. After a while, he realized he was learning more about the Cretaceous Age from this single creature than he'd ever learned at school – "but it's all a bit exhausting" ... However, he quickly put this comment from his mind, in case it offended.

After climbing steadily, Peter noticed the trees had thinned out. Boulders took over, lying in great limestone slabs. Behind these was the entrance to a gigantic cave, its black mouth swallowing light that filtered in.

"Come inside. Don't be afraid. It's called Woo-Kee."

Peter followed. There were ferns everywhere; all dif-

20

ferent shapes and varieties, with moisture from the cave roof dripping on to their leaves.

"Woo-Kee!" he shouted into the mouth.

"Whoooooo!" answered his call, as a great white owl swept out and glided away.

"Careful doing that," the woodlouse warned. "Never know what you might call up!"

It was wonderful to be in the humid cave, so cool after all the heat.

"Yes, the temperature's always the same in here, no matter what's going on outside."

The sun's rays reached into the cave-mouth in a series of steeply sloping shafts which sparkled pools of light on the slippery stones and allowed Peter to see where he was going. At the far end of the cave the entrance narrowed, then curved sharply before widening to a second cave. Peter followed carefully, but every pebble he disturbed echoed loudly.

He was staggered by the beauty of the second cave. It was vast. From a small opening high above, light filtered through bank after bank of fern, eventually reaching the ground in a mottled carpet. Amongst the ferns, little finch-like birds were piping trills and runs. As his eyes grew used to the gloom, Peter saw stalactites and stalagmites; fantastic sculptures reflected in a dark pool in the centre.

"Water wells up all the time from ever so deep. Taste. It's clear. Sweeter than rain."

Peter did so, bending down to cup his hands. Then he took off his T-shirt and used it as a flannel to wash his face and arms. It felt marvellous, and the T-shirt, when he put it back on, clung coolly to his skin.

"The dinosaurs know nothing of my cave. They always go to the lower one by their track, next to the sea. Dinosaurs don't like difference."

"The sea? Dinosaurs?"

"Noisy creatures: far too large, most of them. See them if you must – I'll do other things." With that, the woodlouse scuttled away into the dark.

Outside, Peter discovered a wide, flat plateau below which water gushed from the cave in a sheet before falling to a rockpool hundreds of feet below. Then it wound in a silver ribbon down through a wooded gorge and, beyond this, Peter was delighted to see the sea. Its bleached-out horizon melted in a heat haze with the sky, making a wide gap through a line of mountains. Far to the left, some gigantic birds flapped in an ungainly flock. Peter squinted, trying to make them out. "Dinosaur birds! Maybe they're a kind of pterosaur. I must find out."

He started to scramble down the pathway through the trees – past oak, sycamore, walnut, ash. It was almost the same as walking in the country at home. But not quite . . . For he had caught sight of three snails, so colossal they almost reached to his knees. They were probably there for the water, as he could hear a slurping, squashy noise as they drank. Although they looked very handsome, with pale pink and brown spiralled shells, they smelled foul; and their slime-trails, woven across the rock, looked too slippery to cross. Peter would avoid them; he couldn't be sure they were friendly.

The waterfall tumbled and gurgled off to one side before disappearing suddenly through an opening in the ground. In the silence, Peter became aware of soft, scuffling noises through the trees. Was something following?

He walked faster, almost treading on a snake which slithered silently away. Something – or more than one thing – was definitely stalking him; he could hear squeaks, first from behind, then in front, then to the side.

Round the next corner, there they were; a group of furry rodent-like creatures, almost as large as himself. And they were blocking his way. Peter hesitated, then doubled back; but the rodents darted easily around, their ropy tails swinging and coiling.

"Maybe they're only playing? I'll walk on as if I'm not afraid."

But shrew-like eyes glinted; a circle formed. One started a clucking noise at the back of its throat, which was taken up by the whole gang, closing in.

Peter shouted fiercely. He swung round and round, holding his sandwich box wide. For a moment they backed away, and he rushed the remainder of the path. He could hear them right behind, but visible through the trees was the pale limestone wall of the lower cave – and, beyond that, a sandy beach. "If I dash the last few yards to the open, maybe they'll stay in the trees."

But the furry monsters were as quick, and scampered in front with ease. Then Peter realized they were teasing; they could outrun him with no difficulty. They began to jab him, plucking at the jersey round his waist.

Desperate now, Peter charged headlong at the ones blocking the path, managed to break through, and again raced forward. He stumbled heavily over a root, and was sent bowling straight out on to the beach. Fine sand covered his T-shirt and face. Through a fit of coughing,

23

he saw the rodents racing out after him. The jabbering changed to strange triumphant calls, like chalk scraping on a blackboard. Then they were all over him; hot breath sniffing, muzzles slobbering on his arms, sharp teeth closing on to his legs.

He curled up into a tight ball, protecting the back of his neck with the sandwich box and bringing his knees up to shield his chest and face. If they were going to eat him, they certainly weren't starting on his front.

There was a loud bellow, noisy thundering feet. The lash of a tail scythed through the air above him. Squeaking turned to yelps. Peter lay there, immovable, eyes clenched tight. He pleaded, "Let me go home. Please! This isn't fun any more."

Scampering feet died away. Two jets of hot damp air shot on to his head. A tongue ran gently down the hands covering his face, followed by a whimper, "Not dead. Not really."

Then Peter felt his whole body turned over. It was a powerful movement and he could no longer stay curled up, so he opened his eyes and looked straight into a greenish face, the same size as his own; a face with large round eyes, full of wonder and concern. "See! Not dead at all. Saved it."

Peter gasped. The face was joined to an enormous neck. That was joined on to a gigantic body – and this was only the baby. The adult dinosaur, the mother, stood near by, placidly looking on, her great grey tail swishing from side to side.

Chapter Four

THE DINOSAURS

"What have you found, Segui?"

"A woodlouse," said the smaller dinosaur, "because it curled up."

"I'm not," Peter answered indignantly, although his voice trembled.

"Not scared of *you*. You screamed, didn't roar. You're little. Open mouth – look – not many teeth."

It nudged Peter's mouth open, nibbled at his ear and smelled him all over. This tickled, but still he shrank back and could only peer through his fingers in terror at the tremendous creatures.

"It's all right. Won't eat you. You're yellow and blue, not green. Ghastly poisonous is yellow and blue. No, saved you because of the picture of me on your horn." It sniffed the cartoon dinosaur on the side of the sandwich box which Peter still clutched. "Is it your horn? S'not very sharp."

"It's not a horn, it's plastic," Peter explained, feeling a little braver.

"Plastic! Nice name – I want to be called Plastic."

"Don't be afraid, we won't eat you," said the massive form of the mother dinosaur coming over. "I'm Jahunda and my baby is Segui."

Peter was relieved he wasn't to be eaten. "Thank you both for saving me. I'm Peter."

"Peter!" squealed Segui. "Nice name – *I'm* called Peter!"

"You'll stay as Segui. We named you while you were still in the egg, and Segui you'll stay."

Peter laughed. Segui was delightful, mostly a blotchy-grey colour with pale cream edged with blue on his belly and under his tail. Streaks of dark grey marked his snout and surrounded the large brown eyes.

"Are you brontosaurs? You're very like brontosaurs, only they said they'd more or less died out."

"No, *Opisthocoelicaudia* – but there are very few of us left."

Jahunda now bent to smell Peter. Her massive form towered above him, but he tried not to cringe; and as she lowered her small head, her eyes wrinkled into folds. He saw they were kind – he could look right into them – and full of experience; a little sad as well. Jahunda's breath was hot and sweet, but in case the tickling started again Peter stood up quickly and dusted the sand off his clothes.

"He walks on back legs!" squealed Segui. "Poor thing! Got no tail! I like his crest."

Peter took off his cap and slapped away the sand. At that, both Segui and Jahunda took a step backwards. They were most impressed.

"Take off crest! Again! Again!" cried Segui happily.

Peter obliged, until he felt more relaxed in their presence. Soon he found the courage to walk nearer. Then very slowly he reached out to touch the baby dinosaur. Its skin was soapy and smooth to stroke. And then, when he plucked up courage to touch Jahunda, her skin was rougher. It had the same creamy-blue colouring as Segui's underneath, but the rest had mellowed to more adult, darker colours. They formed a wriggly pattern all over her back, and were in lovely shades: slatey-blue, olivey-green and a very dark steel grey.

For some time they studied one another with great interest; then, "Come along with us. You look as if you need a drink and wash," observed Jahunda. "We've come from the High Plain to go to the lagoon. Segui usually travels in my shadow. You can travel in between – unless you want a ride?"

"Nnnn, no thank you." Peter looked aghast at the great height of her back, far too frightened of falling off. "But I'd love to join you."

They set off down the well-trodden track. Peter was both thrilled and overawed to be between such massive creatures. Jahunda and Segui's legs were huge pillars that made baggy folds when they bent their knees. But they moved with such grace. "Dinosaurs aren't clumsy at all," Peter declared.

It was almost the hottest part of the day, and the sun beat ferociously down from nearly overhead. But Jahunda cast a colossal shadow to keep him cool, and Segui made a smaller one to accompany him on the other side. As they moved along, the great bulk of dinosaur bodies rocked gently from side to side, with a slight creaking as skin rubbed against skin. Dinosaur smell was very strong: a steamy mixture of damp straw and mushrooms – and a bit of old sock. Peter enjoyed walking in or around various footprints left by previous dinosaurs.

They passed the entrance to the huge lower cave Peter had seen from the footpath. Clumps of tall horsetail fern shaded the mouth so you couldn't see inside. Jahunda read his mind. "That's called Hedder Cave. You must always sniff to check it's safe before carrying on." Peter sniffed.

Soon, glimpsing between their legs, he saw the lagoon, lined with tree ferns, willows and weed. From the far margin a low mud delta, shimmering like a mirage, seeped its way out in curling fashion to join the sea. For some while now Peter had become aware of a honking noise. Jahunda and Segui increased their stride as this grew louder, and he had to speed up to stay with them. Before long, however, Jahunda stopped and urged them over to one side. "We're too late now to be first," she sighed.

Behind them, along the track up to the High Plain, coming from a dark pine forest beyond, Peter could see an enormous dust cloud which turned quickly into a troop of duck-billed dinosaurs thundering by. The hooves on their powerful back legs were stepping in time as they pounded the ground. Heads flashed past sporting ornate crests of greens, yellows and scarlets which bobbed up and down. The younger ones ran in the centre for safety.

Peter cowered behind Segui's legs as the ground-shaking cavalcade dashed by.

"I'm afraid we're too late to drink. We usually beat them to it. Those hadrosaurs won't let us in now. They're such a greedy, selfish lot. They eat all the weed and muddy it up for everyone else."

"Oh dear! That's my fault," Peter apologized. "I slowed you down."

"You were saved – and that is more important. We'll go to the second lagoon beyond the headland; and when we pass the ankylosaur, I'll ask if the coast is clear. Come on, then."

"Wait! I *shall* have a dinosaur ride – then I won't slow you down. Only I was a bit scared before ..."

"Travel on my neck then, instead of my back, and I'll make it low."

Jahunda bent her head right down so he could climb on; then she lifted it and crooked it so that he could steady himself with his hands around her neck. Up there it was terrific; kind of scary *and* fantastic.

As they passed the lagoon, first one hadrosaur, then all of them looked up, staring enquiringly as Peter rode high on the dinosaur neck. Some had weed-bunches stuffed in their beaks which hung down dribbling; others chomped sideways, gobbling huge mouthfuls wrenched with webbed forehands from the muddy depths. Above their heads, clouds of insects, disturbed from the water, made little swarms of shade. The water was already muddied completely.

"There seems to be more of those duck-bills every time I look," sighed Jahunda, "and they all copy one another. See! They all want to be in the same place – though there's plenty of room."

"Bog-Brains! Cress-Heads!" Segui shouted out.

"Bog-Brains! Cress-Heads!" yelled Peter from his position of safety.

At once a honking, whistling and trumpeting broke out. Some blew bubbles or snorted like geysers, others made fluting noises or sprayed jets from their long nostrils.

Peter laughed. "How clever of them to blow those sounds."

"They are actually *not* very clever. We only tolerate them because they're useful. They've excellent eyesight – and those noses can smell Tyrannosaurus rex a mile away, long before we do – though our own sense of smell is pretty good."

Peter thought it could be that the duck-bills outnumbered them 20–1, but now they had passed the lagoon and reached some steep limestone cliffs. It was below these that a ferocious creature tore out from a wild area of scrub, with head lowered to challenge them. Peter clutched Jahunda's neck but when the ankylosaur saw who it was, she stopped short.

"Sorry. I'm guarding my eggs and you can't be too sure." She spoke with a nutty voice through a parrot-beak.

Jahunda bent her neck so that Peter could get off and be introduced. Again he was most unsure. This ankylosaur was a great, broad, brown dinosaur, protected with knobbly armour-plating, and as shiny as a rubbing of boot polish. Courageously he went over to pat her, but when she thumped her heavily clubbed tail on the ground in greeting – as if she were a dog – he jumped aside as fast as he could.

"Sorry. Can't help my reflexes. It's only self-defence – I'm really quite soft underneath, though no one will ever turn *me* over . . ."

"Ankylosaur, is the second lagoon safe today?" asked Jahunda. "Is the coast clear? We haven't drunk yet; we're terribly thirsty."

"Well, a kill *has* been made at the entrance to the

gorge. I heard the roar at dawn. Teeth were scattered everywhere. Tyrannosaurus rex hates swallowing teeth, so it must have been him."

'Good, we'll be safe then. His tremendous stomach will need to rest for a few days before the next meal."

"Tyrannosaurus rex killed my father," said Segui, sadly.

"Segui can't really remember that. He was far too young. But yes, he died protecting us."

Peter saw once again the sadness in Jahunda's eyes as she stretched down to offer him another ride, and now he understood why it was there.

The heat was growing stifling, so they headed towards the water at a faster pace. But a cold shadow passed across the sun, and a screeching had them all looking up. Peter shielded his eyes to see the awesome, jagged shape of a pterosaur gliding towards the headland. The screech was made to a second monster pterosaur following behind. Peter was about to comment on their tremendous wingspan when Jahunda halted. Behind them, Segui was staring fixedly, not at the pterosaurs but beyond the reptiles into the sky. He was moaning and shaking uncontrollably.

"No! Not again!" Jahunda cried, turning back. "This happens more and more."

"Coming from the sky. Soon, soon. So scared," Segui cried, in a difficult breathless whisper.

"He waits for something dreadful to happen, and is unable to stop it. At night he calls from his dreams, and he is terrified. He says it's a warning. I find him staring; searching and searching among the stars."

"Mustn't come. Mustn't," Segui whimpered.

Jahunda circled her child uneasily. "He says that over and over again – trying to make it not happen. It is a foretelling, he says, for us all. We don't know what to do."

Peter felt useless. He didn't know how to help. So he stroked Jahunda's neck. He had seen her face turned towards Segui, and it had grown careworn and rather haggard.

Jahunda nuzzled Segui under the chin and nipped gently at the folds on his neck until eventually he came from his trance, and was calm. Soon he seemed to have forgotten all about the event. He rubbed against his mother's horny skin, and they were on the move again.

Chapter Five

THE LAGOON

They walked, at first in silence, but soon rather noisily, as Segui was back to his usual playfulness, jumping in and out of his mother's shadow. From the side of the track tiny creatures in the bushes squeaked but nothing ventured out. Everything scuffled away when it saw Jahunda or heard vibrations from their feet. Immediately ahead, the limestone cliffs curved outwards to form a headland over the sea, and the track turned out to meet it.

Once they reached the sea, a welcome breeze blew in a clean, salty odour. Flocks of sea birds gliding parallel to the shore dived together over shoals of fish. The headland ended in a sheer cliff face with an overhang that leaned precariously. On the summit, perched in a long line, were the pterosaurs, come inland to nest among the crags. Some had wings folded; others held them wide to dry before launching from the cliff edge to spear the fish at sea level, or snatch at flying fishes leaping in silver arcs.

At the tip of the overhang, a few fig trees curled their roots round the rock, like fingers gripping for a hold. Hanging from their boughs, strange black, crinkly bundles slept as they swayed gently in the breeze. They were the fruit bats, folded upside-down, draped like huge parcels in their own leathery wings.

When the dinosaurs reached the shade of the overhang, Jahunda lowered her neck for Peter to get down, and for a while they rested among the chunky boulders which had fallen from the outcrop and lay strewn into a beach. Peter peered into the shallow, incurling waves at the gently wafting sea crinoids. And while Segui and Jahunda began to eat these water lily flowers, Peter poked about in the bleached white sand, finding ammonites and other outsize empty shells, coiled in wonderful designs.

Soon the crinoids were too salty to eat; the dinosaurs needed fresh water at the lagoon. Jahunda sniffed the air with care before they left: there was a dangerous darkly wooded gorge just the other side of the headland. But it smelled safe.

"Race you to the lagoon!" she snorted. Segui shot off after her, and Peter ran as fast as he could. Frogs croaked and jumped into cycad ferns and bullfrogs bellowed and settled low in the reedy mud as the racing creatures thundered to the lagoon. Several giant tortoises heaved themselves up and hobbled off to hide in the thick clumps of club moss, and some tiny smooth-skinned dinosaurs, no larger than chickens, scrambled away screaming into the water willows.

Jahunda and Segui stretched far into the centre of the sparkling pool, lifting water with their heads and allowing it to trickle over their eyes and down their necks. They drank for a long while until their thirst was quenched. Peter drank from the edge, but watched with interest as the gulps of water made spasmic waves down the dinosaur throats.

Next it was Jahunda and Segui's turn to watch fascinated as, after he had put his disc safely inside his sandwich box, Peter appeared to shed his skin, wash it, and hang it out in bits to dry. Then they waded deeper into the cool to feed. But when Segui saw Peter not eating, he grabbed a mouthful of dripping weeds and stuffed it encouragingly into his mouth which Peter had stupidly opened to say, "No thank you."

A resounding crash soon stopped their feeding. Peter looked beyond the gorge to a plain, and was thrilled to recognize a large group of triceratops. Two of the larger males had stopped browsing the gingko trees to charge at one another. They seemed to use their heads like battering-rams. "Wow! Now I know what colour they are!" he thought. They had exceedingly smart, dark yellow-and-tan hides, and behind their three horns was a kind of solid, horny ruff.

The females took no notice of the fighting and calmly continued to shear the gingkos with their beaks. Peter noticed the tree clumps had been eaten around the base to a much higher level than by ordinary cattle.

Jahunda took no notice either. "That's male rivalry to get females in the mating season. It's mostly for show. They're not really fierce – unless threatened," she said, and she closed her eyes, snorted, snaked her long neck under the surface, mixed water and sediment into a rich creamy ooze, then rolled her huge body over in the mud. After that, she lay on the bank out of breath while steam rose from her flanks. Peter looked surprised; he didn't know that dinosaurs had mud-baths.

"First you cover yourself with ooze," she instructed. "Then you let it dry to a hard skin which cleans you when it crumbles off. Try it."

"You look like a pastry case," laughed Peter, when her mud was set.

"Pastry! Pastry! I want to be called Pastry!" squealed Segui in delight, and he rolled such a thick layer of mud over himself that, as it dried, it broke off in great chunks because he wouldn't keep still.

Peter rolled for ages, squeezing the ooze between his fingers and toes. As it dried it made his hair shoot into tufts. But he wouldn't keep still either, so it cracked all over, and as he washed it off it became more and more slippery. But afterwards, his skin felt tingling and marvellous.

They lay in the warm air next to the lagoon where the water had sunk into the pits and marks made by previous creatures going to drink. The hum of insect wings filled the air. Peter felt happier than he had ever been. His mind filled with thoughts. He thought how nice it was the way Jahunda was so patient and encouraging – not like his own mother who always fussed and bothered. Scientists were always saying that dinosaurs had small brains, but they were wrong. Dinosaurs thought differently, that was all.

Jahunda's always aware of everything around, he said to himself. She senses things. She smells into the direction of the wind as if the smells were visible. She probably forgets things if they're no longer important, so wouldn't need a larger brain – but I suppose that's why she can't understand Segui's strange, warning fear . . .

36

Jahunda can measure with her body: she can lift up a great leg delicately to scratch in an exact spot behind her head. She saves her massive energy for when she needs it and doesn't crash about all the time roaring like in the films. And dinosaur tails are always made to look so stiff inside museums, when really they can move quite well. Jahunda's tail goes on for a long way behind her, but because it's thick and strong at the base and slender at the tip, she can curve it up and flick large flies from her body so expertly that they sail through the air stone-dead.

As if to illustrate his thoughts, Jahunda diverted the line of white ants which was marching single file across her body with the tip of her tail, then gave herself a rasping scratch with a toe where they had been.

But one of the giant tortoises had ventured back, and was now staring at Peter so unflinchingly that he had to stop his thinking.

As for Segui, he had already got up, bored with being still, and was on the margin of the lagoon trying to jump off the ground with all four feet at once – but he couldn't quite manage it.

"Can you swim, Peter?" asked Jahunda.

"Yes."

"Then why don't we go to the sea and play? You could carry your skin, crest and horn if they make you too hot."

Chapter Six

TYRANNOSAURUS REX

As they left the lagoon, the dragonflies flew back, shooting in sudden bursts from one level of air to the next on pale papery wings, and some large hard-cased beetles droned in low over the water. The main heat of the day was past; the sun sank deeper in the sky. Over the sea it sent stardust sparkles on to the two great beasts and the small boy playing in the foam. Peter slid down Segui's tail and Jahunda smacked the surface with hers, sending up water showers. They played expertly and were so gentle with him.

Then all at once, in a streak of green and brown, a massive sea monster reared its head above the brine. Peter screamed and clung to Segui's neck.

"It's all right! It's only Archelon the Sea Turtle. He wants to join in. He usually plays with us."

Now the games increased in pleasure as Archelon made his shiny back into a terrific water-slide. They played until the afternoon sun turned a watery orange and was drawn down behind a bank of cloud. It was only when the sun re-emerged below the cloud and poured golden light on to the sea, that Peter realized it was getting late.

Suddenly he panicked. Supposing he'd been recalled while he was bathing? He had left the disc on the beach in his sandwich box. What if the disc had gone back without him?

Quickly he slid down Jahunda's neck, tumbled into the water and raced through the foam to the shore. If it *was* too late, he would remain in the Cretaceous Age for ever. "Then I definitely would be the very first Man," he thought bitterly, "and they'd have to rewrite the whole of history – once they discovered my remains."

Peter wrenched open the sandwich box. The disc-case was still there. Was the disc inside it? Yes, it was! Feeling sick and shaking, he hastily pulled on his clothes and put the disc, unwrapped, inside his pocket – he wasn't taking any further chances. "Of course, if it had gone back without me, I suppose it would've taken back all my clothes. Poor Ivan, can you imagine just a heap of jersey and jeans arriving in the Natural History Museum? Imagine the look on his face!"

But Peter's laugh was shattered, and the grin froze on his face at a sound so terrible that the whole headland echoed it back in disbelief.

Peter panicked. He was alone, in full view of whatever it was. The pterosaurs rose like a black sweep of witches, flapping and screeching above the overhang. Then the alarm was taken up by the ankylosaur, who clubbed a warning on the ground. From further along, the herd of hadrosaurs carried the alarm, sending it out in an ear-splitting cacophony of whistles and honks.

"Jahunda! Segui! Help!" Peter screamed, as the dinosaurs splashed from the sea.

A second roar had revealed a monster rearing up in

strident colours of orange, brown and flame. He was in amongst the triceratops, threatening the herd. The females were encircling the young, while the large males rushed up and down in front of Tyrannosaurus rex, trying to distract him by lowering and tossing their heads. And they bellowed and bellowed so that Peter had never heard anything so fierce and full of power in all his life.

Peter flung his arms round Jahunda's neck as she lowered it for him. "Pick me up! Pick me up!" he implored.

As the dust of the stampede settled, Peter saw that the smaller males and larger females had formed a circle facing outwards, with the young safely enclosed. The dominant males had successfully confused the oncoming carnivore by their to-and-fro action, and they themselves now joined the circle, so that whenever the attacker attempted to breach it he was forced back by an array of horns. Very quickly, the roars of terror turned to roars of frustration as the attacker, seeing he could get nowhere, lumbered off down into the gorge, and the roars faded away.

"Hurrah! Hurrah!" Peter cheered. "The triceratops have won!"

"Hush! Quiet! Stupid one! Don't you see, if he hasn't made a kill *there*, he will try somewhere else – maybe even *here*. Come on, we must make for the overhang before he sees us, and hide in the safety of the rocks. It's our only chance. Ankylosaur was wrong. That roaring she heard must have been a kill made by something else – unless of course he's got himself a mate. No kill means that he will still be hungry and will strike again."

Even as she spoke, a loud, hungry-sounding roar came from much nearer, and although Peter was far up on her neck, he felt Jahunda shudder. Then they were galloping flat out along the shore. Sea water rose as steam from Jahunda's hide. Her neck was slippery and smelled of fear. Peter tried to cling on, but he kept sliding down. If he swung below her neck and let go he would be trampled underfoot.

Another roar came from very close, and there was the beast crashing through the undergrowth at the bottom of the gorge. He had seen them and was trying to cut them off, striding along so fast that his colours blurred in streaks of scarlet and orange. His colossal head was held out in front, balanced by powerful back legs and a massive tail which he held horizontally behind.

They were too late: Tyrannosaurus stood there, barring their path and swishing his tail from side to side. Jahunda stopped suddenly and lowered her neck for Peter to get off so that she could fight. First she got Segui behind her, then stood her ground, snarling. But her row of vegetable-eating peg-teeth were powerless. Tyrannosaurus rex reared up and opened colossal jaws to reveal a battery of long, serrated front teeth and, behind those, a thicker band of crushing-molars. Jahunda also reared, and stamped her thick, trampling feet so hard that the ground thundered.

The monster backed away, bending his massive head towards Peter, who felt a blast of hot, sickly breath smelling of ancient meat. Bravely, he lashed out at the dripping nostrils with his tiny sandwich box. The hideous jaws closed over the case, ripping it easily from his grasp, then crunched it eagerly down. But some sharp splinters of plastic pierced his throat and stuck in his gullet. The great beast looked surprised. He glared at Peter, reared again and tried to spit them out. Peter saw his melted chocolate bar dribble between the teeth and over blood-red gums. There followed a dreadful retching until most of the sandwich box lay in a coughed-up heap on the ground.

In a greater rage than before, Tyrannosaurus swung towards Peter's yellow underbelly, the soft fold of skin around his middle. Peter felt a pinch as tremendous teeth closed on his yellow jersey. He wriggled and twisted desperately, managing to loosen the sleeve just as it was wrenched from him, spinning him round out of reach. Tyrannosaurus rex stuffed this new meat into his mouth and attempted to eat it, but it got caught in his teeth and was dry and fluffy. Disappointed, he tried to cough it up.

"Hurrah! Horn is sharp! Skin is horrid poisonous!" cried Segui.

Tyrannosaurus stopped coughing, gurgled, and went for the small, plump baby. Segui stood rooted to the spot while the beast hooked the two fingers of his front legs into his shoulder to steady it, ready to plunge his teeth in and tear a tender morsel from the flank.

Jahunda seemed unable to move. Her mouth opened but no sound came out.

"No! No!" screamed Peter at the top of his voice. "Don't you touch him!"

The creature let go of Segui and roared at Peter. He would eat this annoying creature whole, distasteful or not. Foul saliva shot out in readiness as the dreadful face came close for a second time.

In split seconds Peter tried to think. "I have my penknife but that would be a pinprick. That only leaves the disc. Of course! Why didn't I think of it before?"

Segui, cowering behind Jahunda, saw Peter wrench the shiny disc from a fold in his skin. Then, using the low, fierce, yellow light of the sun, he directed its glinting rays straight into the creature's eyes. They flickered and closed – and suddenly Jahunda could move again. She read what Peter was doing, saw her opportunity, turned her huge body round and, with her full strength, swung her tail smartly. With a crack that whiplashed through the air, she cut a great weal across the creature's face.

Tyrannosaurus howled. The gash was deep. He opened his eyes to search for his opponent, but again Peter flashed the disc in his eyes, and again Jahunda slashed across his face, stinging his eyes and lacerating his nose. Blinded and seared with agony, the creature curled in upon itself.

"Quick, Peter! Climb on and we're away. Come on, Segui! Come on!"

Only once did Jahunda pause to look behind her. She saw the great carnivore lumber towards the gorge, roaring with pain. He would not trouble them again.

They stopped only when they reached the first lagoon. There wasn't a creature in sight; everything had fled in terror. Jahunda would bathe Segui's cuts and then they could drink and rest. Exhausted, she lowered her neck for Peter to get off, and they were about to thank him for saving them when he disappeared.

Chapter Seven

THE OTHER MR PHILLIPS

"Peter, you've come back!"

"How long was I gone?"

"For about eight seconds."

"Only eight seconds?"

"Yes."

"But I was away for ages – and look, my watch says seven thirty. I really did go, you know. You don't believe me, do you?"

"Oh, but I do. You are quite, quite different."

The little boy who, only a few seconds before, had seen Peter disappear, started to yell his head off. His mother came rushing over.

"He isn't there! He isn't there!" he bawled, pointing accusingly at Peter. The mother looked at Peter uncomfortably and said, rather roughly, to her son, now purple with exertion, "Come along, Gerald. This has all been far too much for you. We're going home."

Peter felt exhausted. His knees were trembling. He wanted something to eat and drink. "Have you got any money on you, Ivan?"

"Loads."

"Let's go to the canteen then and I'll tell you what

happened. How do you mean, I 'look strange'?"

"Well, for a start you're sunburnt all over a bright red. And, well, you look much older . . ."

"Oh, no! I've not gone grey? I wasn't away *that* long?"

"Don't panic! I don't mean wrinkly kind of old . . . but older in your eyes. More . . . sort of wiser."

They stopped in the washroom so Peter could consult the mirror. Behind him as he walked trailed a long, thin line of Cretaceous sand. His reflection showed the state he was in, and he took a long time to clean up and wash all traces of the dinosaur fight away. At last he was more like his usual self, except for the sunburn.

"Don't worry, the red will soon turn brown."

"But my cap's faded – and I've left my jersey and my sandwich box behind. Mum'll be livid."

"Why don't you turn your cap inside out, goof!"

"Yes, that's better, she'll never notice. It's a good thing I wore my cap or my hair would have bleached."

"That hair hanging over your forehead is definitely paler."

"Too bad. Let's get something to eat. I'm starving."

In the canteen Ivan said he hadn't really worried about Peter being recalled. "You see, I knew you'd have to come back fairly soon, otherwise the Energy Activator would have had to stay in for weeks, for years . . . It would've been highly risky. Also, of course, they knew you'd have to be back by the fifteenth, didn't they? In time to go on your next journey. Perhaps they knew it was only going to be about eight seconds, so they didn't bother to tell us on the disc. The time was insignificant."

"I was nearly eaten and didn't come back at all."

"Well, I'm glad you did, I wouldn't have fancied trying to explain to everybody that you'd got eaten by a dinosaur in the Natural History Museum."

Peter laughed. "The scientist who made the tape, Mr Witkins, must have had a pretty good idea of the difference between Cretaceous time and today's, because I was away for hours."

Peter told Ivan as much as he could about the Cretaceous Age but it was difficult to describe, and he was worn out. Ivan didn't seem to realize how much he'd been through during those eight seconds. Peter took his watch off and readjusted the time to the present. There was a white mark where his watch had been. Funny he hadn't needed to know what time it was while he was away. It hadn't seemed important back there. Now it felt like seven thirty to him – and he wanted to rest. But Ivan kept pumping him for more and more information.

"You smell different, too," he said, sitting next to Peter on the coach going back.

"That's dinosaur smell. I'm sorry if I pong."

"I didn't say it was horrid. I said it was different. It's not that bad. Sort of zoo and cow mixed."

"Well, I've actually ridden on a dinosaur. I also know what dinosaurs eat and what colours they are – even the shape of their dinosaur-pats."

"Wow! What shape *is* a dinosaur-pat?" Ivan was fascinated.

"Round and piled on top of one another in a stack. When they dry they are flat like pancakes."

"Did you know that people collect fossilized dinosaur-pats? They're called coprolites. I'd like to own one more than anything else in the world. Phew! I'm dying to go with you next time. Don't forget to arrange that visit to the Palm House at Kew Gardens for the fifteenth with your mother, and don't forget to ask if I can come – I've got great plans for when I time-travel."

Suddenly he turned to Peter. "You idiot! You didn't bring anything back! I would have brought *something*, even if it was just something rare – a living ammonite or even a small dinosaur. Then I would be rich and famous for ever."

"There wasn't time. Anyway, I didn't think of it. It wasn't like that, I was part of everything there. Not like a tourist getting a souvenir . . . Oh, I can't explain."

"Well, I'm definitely going to bring something back when I go. I'm going to take a huge bag, a suitcase, and fill it with specimens. I'll sell them to the museums and make a fortune. Hey, d'you realize – if you'd been touching one of the dinosaurs – Segui or Jahunda – instead of standing on your own as you said – you might have brought one back?"

"How was I to know when I was going to be recalled? Anyway, there's no way I would bring back Segui or Jahunda. It would kill them."

But Ivan was beside himself with merriment. "Think of the look on everyone's face if a huge, *real* dinosaur had landed with you in the Natural History Museum! Everyone would have gone mad. The staff would be completely frantic. The dinosaur would have thought it was in some kind of dinosaur cemetery with all those fossils around. It would have been smashing! Absolutely fantastic!"

"Shut up! Just shut up! Don't you understand anything? It would be terrible, really terrible for them if they suddenly found themselves here."

"Who is making all this row?" Mr Carter was standing in front of them, swaying in the coach aisle. "You may well look ashamed, Topolski, and you red-faced, Phillips. How dare you spoil the class excursion in this way!"

"Really! Two grown boys like you, shouting like a couple of infants," added Rawley from her seat in the front.

When the coach got back to school, Peter announced to Ivan, "I think I'm going to jog back home, rather than go on the bus."

"Jog back? But you're not used to such violent exercise! You said you're already worn out – you'll kill yourself."

"Precisely! If I arrive home with a red face from jogging, it might just explain my sunburn away."

There was another reason, too. Peter needed to be alone; to think about the day's events.

He began to jog slowly. The evening was cold, and his body felt stiff. As he went along he grew more and more worried. He realized now that he had made a terrible mistake promising Ivan he could come on the next journey. But how could he let him down? Ivan had helped considerably, had housed the activator, had kept watch at the museum, had helped him to understand the program in the first place. No, he could hardly refuse. All the same, he knew that, as clever as Ivan was, he would never understand the dinosaurs and wouldn't know how to talk to them properly in that strange way of think-speaking he could do. Ivan was clever in the wrong kind of way. "And thank goodness I *wasn't* touching either Segui or Jahunda to bring them back," he thought. "They would have been absolutely terrified.

They would have been shut up in some zoo with not enough room. People would have come to gawp at them from all over the world. And they would have missed their weed and lagoons; people wouldn't give them mud-baths to keep their skin supple, swims to cool them if they got too hot. No, they would have pined for their home, and died."

"Peter, you've been running!" his mother said, surprised at his appearance. "And you smell odd!"

"Not running, Mum, jogging. I've decided to take up jogging. From now on I'm going to jog to school and back every day."

"That's excellent. You could do with being outdoors more. Oh, by the way, dear, a man called this afternoon. He asked if a Peter Phillips lived here. He said you'd asked him to come and check a fault in your computer. I said I knew nothing about it, told him you were out – but he insisted that you had asked, so I let him in. I didn't know you were having trouble with the computer. Probably you use it too much."

"I didn't ask anyone to check it. What time did he come?"

"Just after two o'clock . . . about a quarter past."

"What happened?"

"Well, I'm afraid I showed it to him. He checked it over very quickly and could find nothing wrong. He seemed very relieved. He wanted to know how old you were, which I thought odd. But all he said was that you were very young to have such a sophisticated computer. He spoke with an American drawl. Anyway, he seemed to be satisfied. Then he left. "What's the matter, dear? Aren't you feeling well? You look a bit flushed.

Maybe jogging home wasn't such a good idea, especially after an outing. And to do it so suddenly when you're not used to it. I'd better take your temperature to be on the safe side. You're not off your food, are you?"

"No, I'm starving."

"Well, I'll get your supper while you have a bath. You really do pong. You must have trodden in something on the way back."

Peter did have a slight temperature, so after supper he took an aspirin, went straight to bed and was thankful for it.

"Mum, you won't let anyone else in to look at my computer, will you?"

"No, I promise. Now stop worrying and go to sleep."

Before Peter put his smelly clothes in the laundry-basket, he had emptied his pockets, taking out the disc and his knife – and then he had felt the small seed-cone he'd put in there from the woodlouse's glade. "So I did bring something back after all. I'd forgotten." He placed it on the table with his other things. "Tomorrow I'll plant that in the garden."

Peter didn't sleep. He tossed and turned, hot and uncomfortable from sunburn, and worrying about the American visitor.

"If the caller was the other Peter Phillips, he must have come all the way over from Richmond Row, London, Ontario, Canada to trace me. He was expecting to use the time disc himself, and I stopped him. Mr Witkins must have realized by now that it was sent to the wrong address."

When he did eventually sleep, it was only to wake later, covered in sweat, having nightmare thoughts. He had remembered something very important. Wasn't it exactly 65 million years ago that all the dinosaurs died out? If the scientists were accurate enough to send him back to that exact time, and on an exact date, was he meant to discover how this happened? At school they had learned that the cause was very sudden – that they were probably wiped out by an extraterrestrial body of some kind. Could this explain poor Segui's foretelling? Segui was frightened about something coming from the sky. Animals sometimes sense those kind of things – fleeing before an earthquake or hurricane, deserting a ship before it sinks. Maybe Mr Witkins has calculated that something fell on either the 5th, 15th or 25th, but wasn't sure which date? Operation Time Loop is probably a scientific experiment to investigate the past. To see what really happened.

Segui had said, "Soon. Soon. Coming Soon." "It's up to me to think of some way to stop them being destroyed. And that means I mustn't let the other Peter Phillips get the disc back to go on the next time-travel journey. He doesn't know anything about Segui and Jahunda. I've *got* to save them. I can't let them die."

Chapter Eight

THE BABY

Before leaving for school the following day, Peter planted the seed-cone at the end of his mother's cabbage row, where he knew it would get watered.

Peter decided he liked jogging to school; he could think about things as he went along, especially about being in the Cretaceous Age where it was all so free and wild. Here, everything had been tamed or made easy and safe. Sometimes, though, it got *too* wild back there ... Tyrannosaurus rex could strike at any time, or monster rodents for that matter. Wouldn't it be exciting, though, if today you were in danger of being grabbed by a dinosaur, or carried off by a pterosaur looming from the sky ...

GRANNY EATEN BY DINOSAUR WHILE ENJOYING SANDWICHES IN HYDE PARK

or

WARNING: TYRANNOSAURUS REX LOOSE IN CAMDEN TOWN

All at once Peter felt squeezed in by tarmac roads, concrete pavements, houses, cars, and things-one-had-to-be-doing.

At school, he told Ivan about the stranger. "He came,

52

pretending to repair my computer, looked it over, then left rather relieved."

"It must have been the other Mr Phillips come to check if the activator was plugged in for two thirty – to see if we'd twigged about how to use the time loops. But we foiled him, didn't we, by using *my* computer? Haa!"

Their eyes gleamed and they slapped palms together.

"My computer managed to cope with the massive power imput OK but the Energy Activator is still pretty hot. It must have relayed an enormous amount of power. Well, we've got to prevent this other Mr Phillips from getting the disc before I have a go. I suppose it was probably easier for him to find out that we had been using the disc by checking the activator than by going to the Dinosaur Gallery to get back the disc. He wouldn't have known who to look for, and eight seconds was too short a time for him to notice anyone disappearing. It was pretty crowded – and we were out of sight."

"Perhaps we needn't worry any more, then, now he thinks I didn't use it."

Ivan frowned. "Oh, but there's something I haven't told you. He may still twig on to us because it'll probably get in the papers, the local one anyway. Yesterday, at two thirty p.m. precisely, there was a massive power failure in Richmond. It only lasted eight seconds and was hardly enough for people to worry about – though everyone's clock alarms must have gone wrong. The first four seconds were you going, the second four were you coming back."

"It's all right. Mr Phillips would have left in his car by two thirty, before the failure happened. He wouldn't have noticed."

"You've forgotten about the traffic-lights. They would all have failed for the eight seconds – maybe enough to alert him."

"Yes, I suppose you're right. We'll just have to be careful."

"There are exactly ten days, counting today, before the fifteenth. The activator had better stay over at my place for the second journey as well."

"Now he knows where I live, he may try to follow me. I'd better jog different routes or bike in roundabout ways when I go to your house, and I'll keep the disc on me for safety."

"Does he know what you look like?"

Peter thought for a moment. "Yes, he would know. There's that mountain bike picture of us, remember, on my bedroom wall."

During the lunch hour, Ivan came rushing up to Peter.

"I talked to Mr Roberts about time warps after my Advanced Maths class. He thinks that time and space are curved; that it's possible that space can fold back on itself. Different times could run parallel, he thinks, even if they're going at different rates. And I've been thinking – maybe that's why you have to be somewhere at an *exact* time so that you don't miss the right moment to jump across on the time loop. Mr Witkins must have been able to work out what time the Cretaceous Age was running at when it met ours."

Peter was amazed. Sometimes he was *most* impressed by Ivan.

"But I still haven't worked out why you have to be at a certain *place* to travel, except that all three have something to do with ancient Cretaceous times: the Dinosaur Gallery, the Palm House at Kew – though I don't know about the third place, Wookey Hole . . ."

"Well, I did some research on Wookey Hole earlier on. I borrowed the big new atlas to look it up. It's near the Cheddar Gorge in Somerset. It's rather peculiar that where I landed there were two caves with similar names: the giant woodlouse called the higher cave Woo-Kee and Jahunda called the lower cave Hedder. There are several miles between those places today, but maybe there were older caves there in the Cretaceous Age. There was a whole mountain range in front of me with sea around it, and apparently most of the Cheddar area was covered then with a shallow sea. Later, the area got overlaid with other rocks, but a lot of that got worn away again to some of the original rock."

"So maybe you've already gone back to the same spot that we'll be travelling from for the third journey. How strange."

Peter was troubled at the word "we": he had only said Ivan was going on the second journey, not the third; but he would ignore it for now.

Peter felt pleased at their research – until he jogged back home. There everything was spoiled by his mother. She was furious with him because she'd discovered his yellow jersey missing. "I knitted it myself for your last birthday. It's really careless of you. Now I'll have to write to Lost Property at the Natural History Museum. Some honest person may have handed it in – and what about your sandwich box? Where did you leave that? Now tell me the truth, Peter. You've never lied to me before."

Peter paused for a moment, considering.

"A dinosaur ate it. It ate the jersey, too."

His mother looked at his face. It had gone very serious. Suddenly she burst into laughter. "You look as if you really meant it. If only you could see your face." And she collapsed again.

The laughter was catching. Soon they were both laughing hysterically. Peter hadn't seen his mother like this for ages; she was like she used to be in the olden days . . . Then her face changed.

"Oh, Peter! I shouldn't have laughed like that. I think it's going to come. The baby . . . Quick, go and telephone for an ambulance."

Chapter Nine

DINOSAUR RESEARCH

The following day, Peter set up a nursery for the baby in his room. He moved into the smaller study. He had to make his own meals and clear them away. Altogether he felt fed up. He had just known it was going to be like this – everything changed because of the baby.

But when he was allowed to visit the hospital the day after, his mother was cradling the tiny baby in her arms and she allowed Peter to hold her, showing him how to prop her head carefully in one hand.

"I'm going to call her Elsie," she said.

Peter had been led to believe that he was to have a baby brother, so he felt rather confused. A baby sister was a different thing to think about. Elsie was rather sweet and very small.

While his mother was away, Peter dutifully watered the cabbage seedlings – quite often, in fact. Not because of the warm weather, but because the seed-cone he had planted on the end of the row had already sprouted a kind of ferny frond. It was weird the way it was growing so fast. "Maybe time really *was* slower in the Cretaceous Age. Now the fern is growing in our speeded-up time today. I'm sure we *do* live faster."

Peter decided not to tell Ivan about the strange fern. He had said he'd brought nothing back. If Ivan saw the fern, that would mean *he* could bring back Cretaceous samples by the suitcase-full when they went together.

On the third day, his mother returned home. Peter was thankful as this gave him more time for dinosaur research. In the last week of term there was no homework; everyone was finishing their dinosaur class project. Peter caught their Class Master as he strode down the corridor.

"Mr Carter, do you think that it really was a giant meteorite that destroyed the dinosaurs sixty-five million years ago?"

The Class Master ground to a halt. Phillips wasn't usually this keen.

"Why, yes, actually I do. I'm fascinated by the theory. I definitely think it was a meteorite that caused their extinction. An object from the asteroid belt seems to arrive from space every hundred million years, and one of these fell exactly sixty-five million years ago. An iron meteorite – pretty huge and heavy. They're almost sure now it landed somewhere near the Gulf of Mexico, in the South Atlantic Ocean. The explosion must have been catastrophic; so dramatic that even the Poles got reversed."

"You mean North became South and South North?"

"Yes, this has happened in the past, several times. A large magnetic shock, from the impact of an immense body – like a meteorite, striking the earth – could cause the magnetic field to alter. But look, I can't stop now. If you're interested in all this, why don't you stay behind after school. It's difficult to understand, but if you are willing to give it a bash. . . ."

Peter had never volunteered to stay after school. He usually cleared out as soon as he could, but he had to know what might happen to Jahunda and Segui before he could help them. Eagerly he accepted.

"Meanwhile then, here's a dinosaur book which I've just been reading myself. It's pretty interesting."

"Thanks," said Peter, almost grabbing the book. He had seen that it was called *The Great Extinction* and he knew what he was looking for would be inside.

Mr Carter entered the Staff Room in time to overhear Miss Rawlings saying, "Apparently there are two new slang words going round. I overheard someone using them. Bog-Brain is one, Cress-Head the other. I asked one of them what they meant – Phillips, I think it was. He said Bog-Brain meant your brain was soft and swampy, and Cress-Head, that you had no mind of your own so copied what everyone else did. Quite good I thought, eh?"

"That's funny, I've just been talking to the Phillips boy, too. His eyes positively dazzled with eagerness. He's even agreed to stay behind to discuss something for his class project."

"Yes, Peter Phillips seems suddenly to have changed, opened out – become interested in everything. We even caught him yelling at that whizzkid, Ivan Topolski, in the coach, didn't we? None of the others would have *dared*!"

Mr Carter laughed. "He turned in a good dinosaur poem as well; and he's already coloured in the Cretaceous dinosaurs on the class chart – most imaginatively I thought. I definitely see an increase in young Phillips's contribution. I may give him a good report for a change."

Peter read *The Great Extinction* in the corner of the library during the lunch hour. The description of the meteorite was horrendous . . .

If the meteor entered the Earth's atmosphere from outer space, it would take only a few seconds to land. The explosion would be colossal – far bigger than any nuclear explosion, and nothing like a human could have ever heard before. Its shock waves would arrive as a continual roar, causing earthquakes around the world.

Where the meteorite landed in the sea, it would turn into a fireball rising into the sky. The ocean, as it rushed to fill its molten crater, would rise as a waterspout perhaps hundreds of kilometres wide. The sea would be poisoned with acids that would dissolve the chalky shells of many sea creatures. Very few living things would survive in the South Atlantic, and the sky would darken.

The fireball would be followed by a massive tidal wave – a tsunamis: a giant wall of water perhaps hundreds of kilometres high. It would cover all the lagoons around the Atlantic coastlines, drowning the dinosaurs in a salty grave.

Peter read this over and over again until he knew what questions he needed to ask Mr Carter. "How would the meteor affect Jahunda and Segui in England, on the *North* Atlantic coast? How long would the tidal wave – this tsunamis – take to reach them, provided they survived the first explosion? Would it be just long enough for him to save them?"

Peter was on his way to see Carter after school, when he saw Ivan looking for him. "You still haven't set up that expedition to Kew for the fifteenth, have you? Swear to do it by tomorrow. You did promise." And Peter had to swear.

At his talk with Mr Carter, Peter concentrated really hard. The stuff was difficult to follow, but he had to understand, so he started with the most important question.

"How long would it take for the tsunamis to arrive at the English coast, if it fell in the South Atlantic?"

Mr Carter's eyes widened. This boy was really into the thing in a big way.

Peter opened *The Great Extinction*. "You see it says here that at the end of the Cretaceous Age the North Atlantic was a different shape – much narrower, and triangular in shape – but probably as deep."

"Well, now, let's try to find out." Mr Carter got out his calculator and concentrated for a while. "It says here the ocean was about three thousand kilometres wide at the base, and the same from north to south, and probably about four kilometres deep. Now . . . If the tsunamis was travelling at, it says, probably 650–800 kilometres per hour for the eight-thousand kilometres to the English coast . . . I'm not quite sure, but at the most about eight to ten hours."

"And it was a meteor that fell, not something else?"

"Ah! That's the exciting bit. They've got double proof. They've found glass spheres around the impact area that can *only* have come from outer space: they contain no crystals, almost no gas and no water, so they couldn't be formed by a volcano. Also, they've found a strange thin layer of clay, only two centimetres thick, formed sixty-five million years ago at the end of the Cretaceous Age – and this has got irridium in it."

"Irridium?" Peter had never heard of that.

"Irridium is a very heavy white metal – a noble metal – one of the densest of all terrestrial substances. Usually it's only found in the earth's core – so any on the surface must have come from space. It would have taken an iron meteorite of about ten or twelve kilometres in diameter, weighing perhaps two thousand five hundred billion tons, to have supplied this amount of irridium – and that is precisely the size of our meteorite."

"So it *must* have been an iron meteorite that killed them. But what would have survived?"

"Well, not much where it fell. They also reckon a plasma dust from the explosion would have blanketed out the sun for up to two years. It would have been like a long winter's night. The skies would slowly clear as the dust fell – but it would have fallen as acid rain. This, and very little sunlight, would have wiped out many primitive plants and ferns. The dinosaurs that fed on these would die; the dinosaurs that fed on those dinosaurs would die. Yet we know many creatures *did* survive."

"Any dinosaurs?"

"Not many of the larger ones. Small mammals, for example, would hibernate, and not need so much food if their heart rate slowed down. If most dinosaurs were warm-blooded – which they think they were – they would need a lot of food to keep warm, and there wouldn't have been much around. The lack of sun may have made the temperature fall and become too cold. Or the plasma dust may have trapped the warm air, keeping it too hot. No one knows for sure. But I think that's enough for today, don't you?"

"Yes, thank you. That's just what I wanted to know."

Peter felt depressed. That night he worried and worried. How would it be possible to save Segui and Jahunda? Not only would they have to be sheltered from the initial blast, but they would also have to be above the reach of the tidal wave. And they would have to live somewhere where the temperature was all right for them and where they were sheltered from the acid rain, with fresh water and food, until things improved. And . . .

Then the answer came to him so suddenly and simply he could have kicked himself. What on earth was he describing if it wasn't Woo-Kee cave? The answer was there – right where the dinosaurs were.

The giant woodlouse had shown him Woo-Kee and told him that the temperature was always the same. The large central pool came from a deep, fresh underground stream – perfect for bathing and drinking. The ferns could be eaten, and they didn't need much light to grow. The cave would protect them from the acid rain. They might just survive – whereas the lower, Hedder Cave would be flooded by the tsunamis. No, Woo-Kee was the right place.

Chapter Ten

THE MIRACLE FERN

Every day, Mrs Phillips took Elsie into the garden to see the miracle fern, "Ahh-goooogh," she said to it. The baby seemed to be growing as fast as the fern; each required to be constantly fed. Mrs Phillips was totally obsessed with them both. While Peter was jogging back from school the following day, he overheard his mother showing off first her new baby, then her new fern to the next-door neighbour, also a keen gardener. He was intrigued.

"I've seen babies like Elsie before, but as for the fern . . . It's nothing like any fern I've ever come across. It looks quite primitive."

"Isn't it exciting. I've certainly seen nothing like it, and gardening is my big passion. I can't find it in any of my gardening books. And it's growing so fast – almost as if it's obeying a growing speed all of its own. Hello, Peter, dear. That running – I mean jogging – you've started to do is a good idea. You look much healthier on it."

Peter had argued badly with Ivan at school because of failing to set up the Kew Gardens date. He would have to deal with it straight away.

"Hello, Mr Griffin. Hi, Mum. I've been meaning to

ask . . . Can we have a day at Kew Gardens next Saturday, on the fifteenth? Term will have ended, and I'd really love to see the ancient ferns in the big Palm House. As you know, we've been studying the Jurassic and Cretaceous Ages at school and—"

"You could check to see if your new strange fern plant is there," the neighbour interrupted.

Mrs Phillips's eyes began to sparkle obsessively. "Brilliant idea! I could take a leaf with us, and some photos of it, and we could book an appointment with the fern expert on the same day to ask him what it is."

"Could we take a picnic for lunch?" (Peter had to make sure they would be there well before 2.30 p.m.)

"I don't see why not. That's a lovely idea."

"It could be a kind of birthday treat for me, couldn't it, as my birthday's during the following week?"

"I could bake a cake and bring it along. We could have it on a blanket near the lovely Palm House, and we could have candles . . ."

"Can Ivan come? He's been doing dinosaurs with me and needs to see the Palm House for his Jurassic project. Then it would be a proper party."

"Of course, dear. It's your birthday treat – and there's room in the car for three to squeeze in as well as the baby's travel-cot. That's settled then, I'll arrange it. You've always been so interested in plants."

"By the way, Mum, what's the name of the wood that Granny's antique wooden chest is made of? You know, her oriental one?"

"Ah, the one that smells nice? That's camphor wood."

"So that's what those trees were in the woodlouse's glade," he thought. "Camphor trees."

After Mrs Phillips had fed the baby and rested, she at last got round to writing a polite letter to the Lost Property Department of the Natural History Museum. She enquired whether a blue sandwich box had been found; also a hand-knitted yellow V-necked jersey. She enclosed a postal order for the post and package if they were found, and if not, to be put into the Museum funds. She was still upset at the loss; it had taken her ages to knit. Really, young boys were so hopeless with their belongings!

Next she telephoned the seed company where she had bought her cabbage seeds.

"Collins here. Yes, I'm the manager ... A strange seed in your cabbage-seed packet you say? Nonsense! I assure you, madam, every packet is weighed, counted, and sealed scientifically ... No, we're a very reliable firm ... And good day to you, too."

Mrs Phillips sighed. "It must have been dropped by a bird then."

At school, Ivan was delighted about the Saturday excursion. "You see, I've made a special noose, and filled my knapsack with a sharp knife and polythene sacks, and I'm taking a coil of rope."

Peter was horrified: his worst fears were being realized – but there was nothing he could do about it. Ivan refused to understand; sometimes he was so childish. Peter knew that shouting at him would only get him more determined and excited. Ivan's cleverness was definitely the kind that would make him successful today – not back in the Cretaceous Age. If only there was a reasonable excuse to prevent Ivan going. Surely there was a way?

In the middle of the following night Peter awoke with a start. The solution was obvious. Going back to the Cretaceous Age holding the disc between them would be easy enough. But what about coming back? Both of them would have to be holding the disc together when they were recalled. Far too much of a risk unless they held hands throughout the journey – and that was too stupid to think about.

At school, Ivan seemed totally unworried. "How long were you away by your watch? Five hours exactly, wasn't it?"

"Five hours – plus the eight seconds going there and back."

"Then all we have to do is make sure that we are touching for a safety margin of ten minutes on either side of that, and we'll be all right."

"That could be really difficult – even impossible. You don't know what might be happening. Anyway, how do you know we'd be called back the same time as before?"

But Ivan thought it was all too stupid to worry about.

"Well, it's OK by me," said Peter, "just so long as *I'm* the one with the disc on me."

Ivan shrugged. "I don't care. I'm not afraid." He had grown a little jealous of Peter since he had gone on his Cretaceous journey, and it was a nasty feeling he didn't like. Peter had invented the new slang words at school, bog-brain and cress-head. He'd grown more popular with the others. He talked more to them, less to him.

Peter was enjoying his sudden popularity. Maybe the Cretaceous journey really had changed him. He was less afraid of people, he didn't feel quite so boring. He liked having different friends. He got really involved in the end-of-term activities, and that stopped him worrying so much about Ivan time-travelling with him. Perhaps strangest of all, was that Mr Carter, his Class Master, had turned from being a teacher into a friend – a real person: someone he could talk to and discuss things with. Carter had asked him to read his Jurassic poem aloud in class. While doing so, Peter had glanced at the dinosaur-chart to see all the animals he knew so well from the Cretaceous Age, coloured in correctly by him.

THE FIRST BIRD

Archaeopteryx the first bird
Preferred to fly about the sky
Rather than run around
With other creatures on the ground.

With a screech of glee
It launched off from a tree.

Discovering with delight
The fun of feathered flight,
It flapped and soared
Just out of reach of all the roars
And all the snapping, crunching jaws.

It found the ripest crops
In the tall treetops.
And there, out of sight,
Spat out pips with all its might
Blow by blow
On the heads of hungry dinosaurs
Down below.

As the day of the Kew Garden birthday treat drew near, it poured with rain non-stop. Peter was unable to jog to school. Stuck indoors, he found playing with Elsie much more fun than he had thought. She was a terribly good baby, and Ivan was wrong: she didn't cry all the time. He even enjoyed learning how to warm her bottle and feed her. Having a baby sister wasn't that bad.

As for the Cretaceous fern, it was behaving well, too. It had all the water it desired. "If it pours like this on Saturday, I'm afraid Kew Gardens will have to be postponed," said his mother. "I'll have to change my appointment with the fern expert, too. I was asked to take a photo with us, but I can't even use the Polaroid in this perpetual rain."

But when Saturday did arrive, the sun came out and it turned into a perfect warm spring day. Peter sighed with relief until, at 10.30 on the morning of the same day, Peter's father arrived in a taxi, on a surprise visit from Bangkok.

"Isn't it marvellous!" his mother laughed. "He's been allowed paternity leave to see Elsie. He can stay with us for ten whole days!"

Although Peter was overjoyed to see his father, he realized with a sinking heart that the picnic at Kew would now definitely be cancelled. How could he leave the house with his father just arrived? It would be very difficult – but he'd have to do it.

His father was overwhelmed by the baby. He held her, walked around the house with her, made silly noises . . .

"I might as well not be here," thought Peter. "He

hasn't taken any notice of me. He came back to see the baby, not for my birthday."

Peter felt more shut out than he'd ever been. He wandered out into the garden to look at the fern. It was as high as himself now and waved prettily at him in the soft air. "A perfect spring day for Kew," he thought bitterly. "I'll leave right now with the disc and go to Ivan's. They won't even know I'm gone. We'll plug in the Energy Activator Power Pack and get to Kew by train."

Peter went up to his small room to get ready. When he came down, he overheard his parents arguing furiously about the baby.

"But I wasn't consulted, was I? If it was a girl I wanted to call her Jane."

"Elsie is so nice, though. I think she ought to be called Elsie after Granny. Don't you think it suits her?"

"Yes, but I think Jane suits her, too. You might have waited until I came home, then we could have both decided."

"You were miles away, darling, in Bangkok. Besides, she seemed to want to be called Elsie . . ."

"Why don't you call her Elsie-Jane then," said Peter, coming into the room.

"Peter! What a wonderful idea!" his mother exclaimed.

"Elsie-Jane . . . Yes, that sounds absolutely right. Clever boy, Peter! We'll call her Elsie-Jane," said his father, "and then we've *all* decided, haven't we? Oh, Peter, it's lovely to see you again, and so good to be back together like this." He hugged them all together in one huge embrace.

"I suppose my birthday picnic to Kew Gardens is off," Peter said.

"Not on your life," said his mother determinedly. "I've arranged the meeting with the fern expert at twelve thirty provided it's fine. And it is. I'll take the Polaroid photos right now, then we'll be ready to pick up Ivan at twelve o'clock, as arranged. You'll want to sleep after your journey, won't you, dear? You must be jet-lagged?"

"Picnic in Kew? Sounds exactly what I would love to do. Greenery, gentle warm weather. After all that Singapore heat I can think of nothing nicer. Besides, if I feel jet-lagged I can always go to sleep on a rug."

"I'm afraid there won't be room for Ivan to come then, dear. Not with the baby *and* Daddy. It'll be too much of a squeeze. Do you think he'll be very disappointed?"

"But he's got to come. He's really been looking forward to it," Peter panicked. "He'll be completely devastated. He'll—"

Then Peter could have kicked himself. What a Bog-Brain! Of course! This was the perfect excuse for Ivan not to come – and at the very last minute, too. It couldn't have worked out better.

"No, of course not. I'd much prefer Dad to come. I can always go with Ivan another time. I'll ring to tell him. Honestly, it's the best birthday treat I could have – with Dad and Elsie-Jane coming and a birthday cake to eat as well."

"Maybe I'd better ring his mother then. It would be more polite coming from me since I arranged it all. I'll explain everything."

Chapter Eleven

VARIOUS JOURNEYS

An hour later, the Phillips's small car pulled away from 3A Richmond Row. In the front of the car Father drove – mostly on the correct side of the road – with his wife sitting next to him, reminding him to drive on the left. Laid on a handkerchief on her lap was an outsize fern leaf with its stalk wrapped in wet tissue. In the back of the car was a baby strapped into its travel-cot, and next to it a boy clutching a strange disc in his pocket. In the boot were arrangements for a large picnic.

Behind the Phillips's car, another car – a hired, blue Ford, driven by a strange man – pulled away discreetly from further down the road and followed the Phillips's car at a safe distance.

Almost an hour later (after an argument with his parents), a dark-haired, serious-looking boy with spectacles slightly askew, a forage hat rammed well down on his head, a heavy knapsack slung tightly over one shoulder and a coil of rope loosely over the other, left the shed at the back of the Topolskis' house, and departed secretly and stealthily (by mountain bike) on the $2^1/_2$-mile journey that would take him to Kew Gardens.

*

Over 65 million years before the journey to Kew took place, far out in space, on the outer fringes of the Solar System, a large black object, over 10 kilometres in length and weighing over 2000 billion tons, shaped rather like a potato but with a heart of iron ore and nearly as old as the Universe itself, broke away from its thousand-year orbit round the Sun and left under a cloak of methane gas to go on a journey that would take 60,000 years.

It passed Pluto, then Neptune (where great storms surged in its dense blue atmosphere). Uranus sent the object spinning towards Saturn – a great golden orb encircled by rings of ice and dust, where huge storms raged for years at a time. Faster it spun towards Jupiter, the largest planet, where massive storms lasted for hundreds of years at a time. The potato-shaped rock was almost sucked in by it – but instead it slowed it down.

As the temperature increased, the frozen methane cloak began to melt. Weakened by its loss, the potato-object was buffeted through the Asteroid Belt, where large chunks were knocked off. By the time it had passed the Red Planet, Mars, swept by dust storms for weeks at a time, it had become a meteorite, with its methane cloak pushed by radiation and solar winds to a long tail stretching millions of kilometres back into space.

Finally, it found itself on a direct course for a Blue Planet called Earth. Here, no storms raged; only a swirling white cloud of water vapour, under which vast oceans appeared dark against the greens and browns of continents, while brilliant ice-caps reflected sunlight from the poles. Towards this the meteorite sped, at 20 kilometres per second; a tumbling mountain of rock and iron, set on a collision course with Earth.

Ivan was very angry. He wobbled on his bicycle to Kew. This wasn't because of his anger: all the gear he was carrying was having a strong gravitational effect on his balance.

The stranger in the hired Ford following the Phillips's car had only recently arrived from London, Ontario. Therefore he tended to be drawn to drive on the other side of the road every time the car he was following threatened to do so in front. As a consequence, his driving was a little wobbly.

In the Phillips's car, Peter battled with a terrible thought that had just come into his mind, a thought that might possibly send his day at Kew right off course. His friend would be furious that he had gone without him. So furious that he might even consider sabotaging this second journey back to the Cretaceous Age? So angry that he might even fail to plug in the Energy Activator? No, surely not; his friend was still his friend . . . "But I haven't been treating my friend very well lately, have I? I'll just have to take the chance . . ."

"I have the funniest feeling that someone has been following us," said Mr Phillips in his car when they eventually reached Kew Gardens. "But this is the way to stop whoever it is."

Instead of slowing down to park outside the main entrance as other visitors were made to do, Mr Phillips swung into the entrance of the Administration Centre. He gave their name and the gate was opened immediately, allowing them to park in the driveway for their appointment with the fern expert.

The stranger, a bald-headed man with a beard and thick pebbly spectacles, glared at their car before being forced to turn and park outside the main entrance, where he had to pay to get in.

Ivan, slightly out of breath, reached the Lyon Gate entrance to Kew Gardens (the nearest one by bike from Richmond). Quickly realizing that he wouldn't be allowed in there with all his equipment, he crept round the far end of Kew Gardens by the playing fields. There he saw a large branch hanging over the fence. Using his rope and the rest of his equipment, he prepared to climb over.

Chapter Twelve

THE PALM HOUSE AT KEW

The fern expert at Kew stared at the Phillips's fern leaf for a very long time, then gasped at the family's Polaroid photos of the complete plant. Quickly he called in his colleagues. Books and slides were brought out, pieces of leaf put under microscopes. The Phillips family was offered drinks and made comfortable. Eventually all the experts came towards them.

"We think you are on to something quite exceptional here. Your fern is very primitive. There are things similar to it in New Zealand, but nothing quite the same. We do have an exact replica of this, but only in fossil form." Their voices dropped almost to a whisper. "But how could it be a fern that was wiped out at the end of the Cretaceous Age? May we keep this fern frond and do further research? And would you continue to observe your plant's growth carefully and take notes on its development? We would like to come and see it as soon as possible, and—"

"Oh, there's no need for any of that," Mrs Phillips interrupted. "As it's my fern, I would like to present it to the Royal Botanic Gardens at Kew. I was going to do that anyway. My small garden in Richmond is no place for a rare plant like that, and it seems to require so much water. No, it will be much happier here where it can be properly looked after. You may come to collect it as soon as you like."

"Something very good will come from this generous gift, Mrs Phillips. Thank you. We will be able to split it when it's larger and make more. We might even get some hybrids from it – cross it with other ferns. And of course this new species will be named after your family. *Cycas phillipsii* is what it will probably be called."

The Phillips family felt content. They wandered around Kew, then decided to have their picnic. As they fetched this from the back of the car, the stranger – who had wondered where they were and what they had been doing – followed them at a safe distance.

The sun was now the perfect temperature for a picnic. The Phillips family settled themselves on their rug. They had been allowed to place it in the best position outside the beautiful glass Palm House, next to the lake. They ate their sandwiches (but saved the birthday cake for tea).

The stranger, hiding in the bushes not far away, began to feel hungry. His stomach rumbled. He hoped it wouldn't give him away.

Elsie-Jane felt hungry, too, and started to cry, so Mrs Phillips fed her. Mr Phillips became jet-lagged and fell asleep. Peter, who had been keeping a watchful eye on the time, saw that it was twenty past two. He announced to his mother that he was going into the Palm House.

"Then why don't you take Elsie-Jane, too, while I have a little rest for a few moments with your father."

"Well, I can't really. I . . ." He found Elsie-Jane thrust into his arms.

"Now don't be so nervous. She won't bite. Just hold her the way I taught you. Go for a little walk with her in the Palm House. She'll love that. We'll only be outside if she cries. Go on."

And Peter was forced to take Elsie-Jane into the Palm House with him. What could he do? Perhaps someone would hold her for a moment while . . . while what? While he nipped behind a fern frond for a few seconds to disappear? It just wouldn't work.

"Want to come to the Cretaceous Age, Elsie-Jane?" he asked.

"Googh!" she replied.

Peter looked around for a suitable place where he could slip from the pathway into thick greenery, away from the groups of people wandering by. It was almost two thirty – no time to lose. He would put Elsie-Jane down behind a thick fern frond for the eight seconds he was away. She wouldn't really notice if he wasn't there for that long. That was when, to his dismay, he saw Ivan enter the far doorway, looking breathless and wild.

Ivan had been "slightly detained" by a park keeper, who had caught him climbing over the wall. He had only just managed to escape. He spotted Peter with the baby, and raced towards him.

"Oh, no! He's planning to come with me. He mustn't!" Peter whipped round, only to see, to his increasing alarm, a man with a bald head and thick pebbly spectacles running in through the opposite door, also making straight for him.

"Oh, no! That must be the other Peter Phillips, coming to get his disc. What can I do?"

The stranger hesitated, looked confused, stopped

running towards Peter and began to race towards Ivan. The stranger, who *was* the other Peter Phillips, had suddenly realized that he'd been chasing after the wrong person all the time. A boy wouldn't be journeying to the Cretaceous Age holding a baby, would he? No, it was the other one, the boy with the ropes and knapsack – that must be Peter Phillips. Also he definitely recognized him as the second boy riding a mountain bike in the photograph on the wall of the boy's room. It was him who was using the disc. The other boy was only his friend. At all costs he had to prevent him travelling, so he pounced on Ivan. There was a terrific scuffle. Ivan, thinking that this must be another park keeper, struggled violently until he broke free and made off.

With dismay, Peter realized that it was now only seconds before two thirty and he was still holding Elsie-Jane on the pathway. Quickly he put her down and darted into the greenery to hide behind a thick fern.

Elsie-Jane did not like being abandoned so early in life. She let out a piercing yell which attracted attention. The stranger, having reached the baby, hovered over her, confused. Surely this was the baby the other boy was holding? Where was he? He couldn't see anyone around.

"For shame! Putting a baby down like that on the hard ground just so he can look at an exhibit more closely," a stout lady said to her friend. "Pick it up, you scoundrel! You ought to be ashamed of yourself!"

In this embarrassing situation there was nothing the stranger could do but lift the crying infant and carry it towards the exit, looking for its owner.

Peter had already ripped the disc-case from his pocket, opened it and was clutching it in his hand when, to his horror, he saw the stranger making off with the sister who was in his charge. She was now screaming her head off. He must get her back. That was the most important thing. He was about to give chase when he disappeared.

Chapter Thirteen

THE SECOND JOURNEY

There was a roaring. The temperature rose suddenly to 18,000 degrees. In less than two seconds the meteorite passed through the dense outer regions of the atmosphere, forcing a great cloud of plasma in front of it. It was travelling at 20 kilometres per second, and it shone three times hotter than the sun, three times brighter. Its rock started to melt. One second later it filled the sky with a fireball that appeared to be ten times the size of the Sun. Shock waves from the meteorite squeezed back, trailing behind it as it passed through the sound barrier.

The meteorite fell into the Gulf of Mexico, just off the coast. By falling at sixty times the speed of sound, it was travelling too fast for the sea surface to be warned of its approach. The sea began to boil vigorously.

The meteorite struck the ocean's surface and belly-flopped with the force of a hundred million, million tons of TNT. It disintegrated on impact and tore the ocean apart, so that the water leapt upwards with a roar heard the other side of the Earth. The plasma thrust ahead of the meteorite as it cut through the sea, taking two seconds to reach the seabed. As it carved a crater, atoms ionized, electrons were stripped and the meteorite changed into a disc-shaped gas plasma of air, sea and rock – pure energy, expanding instantly sideways and up.

The disc appeared to bounce before rising to form a fire barrel. It filled the entire horizon for three hundred and twenty kilometres, illuminating the sky with flame. Water exploded as it tore in from the surrounding ocean to fill the meteorite's molten crater. And as it met in the centre, eight kilometres of sea leapt into the sky. Like a cloud on a stem, it rose in a colossal water-spout, spreading three hundred and twenty kilometres wide.

In a flash, water, vapour and seabed rock were hurled, superheated, into the atmosphere. Some vanished into space; some entered into orbit around Earth. A huge plume of debris spread sideways in a curtain drawn across the sky. It circled the globe, gradually blotting out the light and plunging the world into darkness. Beneath this curtain, some plasma debris had fallen back on to itself in a great swirling of water and air over the ocean. It created tidal waves, hundreds of metres high.

Slowly these began to surge outwards towards land, followed by a huge roaring, like the end of the world.

At 2.30 p.m. and 4 seconds, Peter fell after the meteor impact, missing it by just over six hours as he was hurtled through time and space into the Cretaceous Age.

He landed in a load of slime and immediately slipped over. The slime was seeping from the side of a great snail shell. The snail had retreated inside, but its shell was cracked all over and the slime oozing from it smelled sickly and cloying. Although it was sheltering Peter from the howling wind, he had to drag himself away from the foul thing. He stood up, clutching unsteadily at a boulder. The air was dense and difficult to breathe, and it was unbearably hot.

He found himself on the limestone ridge just outside Woo-Kee cave. In front of him, out to sea, the mountain range looked as if it was in the process of destroying itself. Above it, a strange dark purple sky was racked with dust-torn bands streaking through dark clouds that billowed high in the atmosphere. Below it, the wind and sea surged together in a churning layer of spray.

"The meteorite has fallen then." Peter tried to look at his watch, but the light was flickering so much and he was shaking so uncontrollably that he couldn't see what it said. When had the impact occurred? How long had he got before the tsunamis? Carter had thought about 8–10 hours. "But if I don't know when the meteorite fell, it could come at any time. And how can I find the dinosaurs in all this? It's impossible." He felt faint and cowardly; but then he steadied himself and thought, "If the other Mr Phillips was supposed to have been able to survive all this, then so can I."

He started to scramble down the small steep track that descended parallel to the waterfall. It was easier to travel beneath the sheltering cover of trees. Although it was dark, his way was lit with a constant flickering of harsh, unearthly colour. The trees trembled like shaking hands trying to protect him above. Under his feet the ground rumbled – a deep rumble, at the very core of the Earth.

"The mountain chain must have taken most of the battering on this part of the coast. It's probably protected this whole headland," he thought.

There was no sign of the rodents – or of any living

creature – and it wasn't too long before he reached the dinosaur track at the bottom. The wind hit him like a hot, wet sock as he came out. Along the track that led back to the pine forests and the High Plain, the trees were down like matchsticks. Streaks of purple and orange shot towards him from the sea mountains, darting shadow daggers on to the rocks. Everything rumbled and shook. Peter tried to run along the track, but it was more of a stumble. The wind gusted from all over the place. One minute he could see; the next he was slapped in the face with wet sand.

By the time he had passed the Hedder Cave entrance and the wooded area beyond, Peter was choking on a cloud of sulphur fumes that caught the back of his throat; but he struggled on, swallowing back stinging tears.

"At this time of day the dinosaurs should have been on their way to drink – if it *is* the same time of day. It's difficult to know with all the sky torn and dark."

Every moment the wind increased in strength. It was a harsh, blinding wind that blew bundles of sea-grass and other vegetation spinning past, or ridged the sand into running ripples, coloured a brick-dust red. Before long, the blowing sand had caked his nostrils completely, making him snort.

The first lagoon, when he reached it, seemed to be boiling like a large bowl of soup. One minute a howling vortex swept the water up, hurling it into a green spiral; the next it flattened into circles of mauve. The willows were bent double, streaked in nightmare shades. Fern fronds flickered before the wind. Then he saw the hadrosaurs. They were crouching among the weeds and rushes while these were torn up around them. He looked for

Segui and Jahunda, but could see them nowhere.

Peter pushed on. He knew that none of the duck-bills would help. Far too recently he and Segui had yelled Bog-Brain! Cress-Head! at them – although now, with everything changed, it seemed like a hundred years ago.

He couldn't understand why he had reached the sea so soon until he realized that it was further in. It raged in a choppy froth, hot and steamy. A strange, chlorine-smelling wind took over from the sandstorm and blew steadily, straight off the sea. Peter rammed his cap down further and dragged his feet along the beach.

Only now did he notice the true destruction. The sea's new beach was littered with bodies of every kind: fish half-eaten, battered coral, broken bellemnites, sea-sponges wrecked, shellfish all crushed. As he walked, the sea spat out further fishy skeletons or hurled ammonites ashore. Then he saw the monster rodents. They had turned scavenger and were tearing and eating the smashed mollusc bodies, enjoying themselves in an orgy of feasting. He felt sick.

To avoid them, Peter tried to break into a run. He had almost passed them when his way was blocked by a large, rubbery obstacle. It was a plesiosaur; a huge one: it must have been at least forty feet long. He had longed to see one of these great marine reptiles, but not shattered like this, with flippers twisted, neck broken, jaws prised open in an awkward, tortured gasp. And, as if to allow him to see the terrible sight more clearly, a volcanic flare gushed up on the horizon, so that he picked his way onwards in a startling new light.

And there was Segui, a wobbling shape in the heat, just where he should not be, at the foot of the overhang

– or what remained of it. But it couldn't be Segui. As he got nearer he saw that this dinosaur looked larger, and it definitely wasn't Jahunda. Then the dinosaur saw him. And it *was* Segui.

"It's Peter! Come back to save us! Too late! Thing fell! Sky's gone purple! Happened like I said! All over now. We hid in here."

To Peter's complete amazement, Segui was almost exultant, totally unafraid. He seemed unaware that a pterosaur lay gasping to death in the fumes right next to his feet. "The sea blew up! A flash! Screaming in the sky! Roaring everything! Brightness everywhere."

"I suppose he's gone like this because the thing that was haunting him all his life has actually happened," Peter thought. "Instead of being frightened, he's relieved."

Peter put his hand on Segui's lowered neck and stroked it. "Yes, Segui. You were right. A great piece of rock fell from the stars. But I'll save you."

"Too late to save. Happened like I said. You didn't come. We waited for twelve moon-fulls."

Twelve moon-fulls? Was it really a year ago? Peter was puzzled. So that was why Segui had grown. Perhaps it was because he had travelled here on a different time loop.

"Where's Jahunda?"

"Won't speak. Won't move. Won't anything. She's in there."

Suddenly there was a rumbling above. Stones fell, followed by a large dark object hurtling through the air. It was a fruit bat. It missed them, but was blown instead on to a thorn branch that had been ripped down. It tried to free itself by stretching its wings, but only succeeded in piercing the membrane further. And there it hung by one extended wing, screeching and swinging in the wind.

Peter shivered. There was no time to clamber over to save it and no time left to talk. But he had to know one thing.

"When did it all happen, Segui?"

"Just."

"When just?"

"After night ended."

"Then we've still probably got an hour or two, if we're lucky. Listen carefully, Segui. A large wave will come. The sea will cover the land. We've got to climb high, to a cave above the cliffside. In there you'll be safe. You must follow where I go. Come on, let's get Jahunda."

As Segui turned, Peter saw that he had been cut really badly on his right shoulder – an old wound opened up. And he realized that it must be where Segui had been clawed by Tyrannosaurus rex.

"Segui, you're hurt. How?"

"A rock fell and cut. From above."

"Then we must leave here as fast as we can. Help me to find Jahunda."

As soon as he entered the cave, Peter saw the danger. The end of the overhang had completely crumbled away, blocking the exit to the second lagoon. He found Jahunda cowered against the cliff face at the back. The sea had almost reached her. He went up slowly, but in the gloom of the overhang she seemed not to recognize him. She seemed confused. It was a different Jahunda from the one he knew. All her composure was gone. The whites of her eyes were enlarged, and she swayed her head wildly from side to side in frantic stabs, using up vital energy.

"Jahunda, it's me, Peter. I've come to rescue you. To take you to Woo-Kee where you will be safe. Please, we must hurry, before the cliff face falls."

But Jahunda had blocked everything from her mind. It was as if she was stuck, as if things were too much for her.

A new tremor began. The whole place was shifting. Jahunda's eyes rolled with fear, her nostrils flared, her mouth hung as if she were wailing soundlessly, and the swinging went on and on.

Segui was now distressed. "Wait. Wait until better."

"There's no time, Segui. The sea's coming in. More rock will fall. She has to follow us."

Peter tried to stop himself panicking. He thought really hard. How could he talk in a way she understood? It was useless telling her about a cave away from their usual route back to the High Plain. Maybe if he could just get them on to the dinosaur track, at least that would be a start in the right direction. After that it would be up to him to get them to leave their usual route and go up to Woo-Kee. But first he must stop her swaying. At home when someone was like that, you were meant to slap them. Yes, that might just work.

"Segui, slap Jahunda hard on the neck with your tail, then order her to follow you along the track. Go on. You must try, or we'll all be killed."

Segui hesitated for a second, then he turned and fetched his mother a great slap on the neck. She stopped swinging her neck in surprise. Then she gave a great wail of despair.

"Segui, tell her that we've finished bathing and are going back up the track. Once she knows she is on her usual route it'll be all right. Say it firmly. Get her to follow. Go on! It's better if you do it."

Segui tried. "It's time to go. Our usual way. Back to the plain. Come along."

He curled his tail around her neck to stop it swinging again, and pulled gently forward the way they were to go. At first Jahunda's legs seemed out of control and her great weight lurched. But Segui picked his way carefully over the boulders, and she followed unsteadily. Once they were outside and on to the path she went with more confidence. Soon they were away from the crumbling overhang.

Chapter Fourteen

THE EARTHQUAKE

It was getting darker and darker. It was almost suffocating to walk in the heavy, sulphurous air. They had nearly reached the end of the beach when Segui saw something ahead: a weird shape, stranded on its back, flailing the air with its flippers. Soon the shape turned into a huge green sea turtle lying helpless, opening and closing its mouth, beseeching from upside-down.

"It's Archelon!" cried Segui. "Save him! Save him!"

To their surprise, Jahunda suddenly took charge as if nothing had happened to her.

"Pull your flippers in," she called. The turtle obeyed. Positioning her two front feet each side of the creature, Jahunda began to rock the shell slowly with her neck, more and more, until with one good heave she nudged it over the right way up. Segui was delighted.

While Archelon collected himself, Peter explained the situation as quickly as he could, warning him that at any moment a great wave might come sweeping in. Then he encouraged them all to hurry along. But now they could hardly see. The sun seemed to be going out, and was being replaced by a dull purple glow from the sky over the sea. It made everything loom in a ghastly way, casting hollow shadows at their feet.

"Follow me," barked the sea turtle. "I'll lead you. I can still see. Keep the wind coming from your left. Keep close together behind me."

With Archelon leading, everything seemed more possible. The little group moved forward, Segui behind Archelon, then Jahunda and Peter at the rear.

Peter was pleased it was dark because, although the track was familiar, he knew the devastation had changed it beyond recognition. In darkness, the animals would travel by instinct and not be put off by what they saw. Peter noticed that Segui was now limping with the pain from his shoulder; but thoughts of the tsunamis, engulfing and terrible, filled his mind, and he constantly urged them on.

Then something happened that changed the whole world. At first the rumbling seemed to come from further away; then it closed in, shaking the earth right under their feet. Peter found he was caught in a terrifying shudder. Seconds later, it was like being sieved. A violent explosion from the mountain range revealed a volcano spouting a plume of orange into the purple sky. Suddenly they could see the way ahead lighter than day. Moments later there was a screaming in the sky as a shower of small glowing particles shot past them at low level. One piece chiselled into the solid rock wall of the gorge, sending out behind it a billow of smoke. The heat was fearful. Seed pods dried and exploded like pistol shots; vegetation crackled. Somewhere over to their right, Peter heard faintly the triceratops bray and thought he could see the ginkgo trees aflame.

Then behind Peter there came a crumbling sound. He stopped dead in his tracks and turned to see the cliff face fall into a heap. "An earthquake," he called, but his voice came out thin and far away and he saw that he had fallen behind a little so that the others could not hear.

Peter was trying to catch up, when right in front of him there was a loud crack and the ground split instantly from the cliffside to the sea. The narrow fissure began to widen, and through it hot, dry steam escaped. Then other cracks appeared everywhere, covering the ground ahead. Through the crazing, more steam curled and crept.

He called out. The others had stopped and were staring in disbelief as the earth opened up and drew them further apart.

"Jump over! Jump!" Segui cried. But Peter was rooted to the spot. On the seaward side, broken pieces of shell spat up from the sand; on the cliffside, one or two geysers started up, throwing out mud that whistled as it separated from steam. All the time the gulf was widening and there was no way round. He was cut off, trapped. And both his friends and the way back were on the farther side.

For a moment the quaking ceased. In the chasm Peter thought he saw molten rock gurgling, evaporating in a thick yellow coil.

"You've got to come," barked Archelon.

"Don't leave us!" Segui cried.

"Jump!" called Jahunda.

But the earth began to quake again more violently, and the crack by now was several metres wide. Over this chasm the separation seemed immense. Boiling stuff and yellow foam were seeping out and spreading all around.

"I can't. I can't," Peter whispered, absolutely terrified.

Now there was a wall of steam between them, and another rumbling made him fall over and cover his face. He no longer thought about the tsunamis; he only thought that he might be swallowed up and boiled alive. Through the sounds he heard Jahunda.

"Grab my tail," she ordered. "You others go on."

And he saw through the steam that she had backed up and stretched her tail over the chasm until the very tip of it rested on his side. Peter crawled towards it and hauled himself on, but it lurched down with his sudden weight and he felt himself slipping over the yawning space. He dug in his nails and clung on for dear life. Then the tail stiffened so that he could pull himself along.

"Steady now, steady. All in good time," she urged. But the sulphur smell of bad eggs was choking his lungs so that he strained for breath. Then a jet of gas made him almost faint. His eyes pricked dry, yet he could feel runnels of sweat sliding down his back. He screwed up his eyes against the fumes and carried on. A rubbery smell was coming from his trainers which were beginning to burn. He winced and gritted his teeth.

Now he was half-way over the bridge. He could feel the skin of Jahunda's tail crackle in the heat – but what he could not see was that she had closed her eyes from the pain and then her nostrils from the smell of burning. She planted her feet more firmly in the ground.

"Hurry now," she urged. "Hurry."

The heat curled around him in great waves. He clawed his way up the folds of skin as fast as he could.

Only when she felt him safe did Jahunda move forward, and only when she knew that he was clinging high on her shoulders did she break into a gallop along the sand.

Chapter Fifteen

HEDDER CAVE

Peter was no longer in pain, nor was there any feeling in the front of his legs. He just held on over the movement of galloping. By the time they caught up with the others Jahunda was exhausted. Segui had lost a lot of blood from his wound which had dried in a crust along his back, and he was limping quite badly. No one could speak; they just carried on behind Archelon, toiling through the heat until they reached the lagoon.

"Thirsty, thirsty," called Segui.

"No. Don't drink," Peter warned. "It may be poisoned, or smothered in sea salt."

Unrecognizable shapes, bloated with strange gases, bobbed up and down on the surface. All the food had been trampled and spoiled, and a great sludge-blanket of green plankton foamed on the margin. Hadrosaurs were blocking their way, though not aggressively. Some were pulling and eating at the weed in panic, as though their lives depended on it. Every so often one would whistle; then they would all join in, lamenting the loss. Most stood round in groups, confused about why the sea had flooded in and poisoned their lagoon.

The hadrosaurs' leader stumbled towards them,

gasping for help through its nostrils. But how could they help? Vaguely Peter remembered that in their class they'd been told that pine needles and fir cones had been found in the stomach of a hadrosaur as part of its diet.

"Leave the lake," he ordered harshly from Jahunda's back. "Go as high on the plain as you can. Into the remaining pine forest. Try to eat the cones and needles. It's your only hope."

The volcano sky now glowered with sulphur clouds tangled into tufts. From these clouds a strange brimstone rain fell, enclosing a stinging dust. Jahunda was plodding along the track when Peter felt her tense up. Then a shuddering passed through her and he saw what she had noticed, slumped right in front of them on the path. It was the ankylosaur lying on her back, dead. She had probably been trying to find them. At the sight of her friend, Jahunda was overwhelmed. She gave a cry of grief, and all her new-found courage seemed to collapse. They gathered round, horrified: the ankylosaur was turned over, all her vulnerable part exposed.

Segui and Jahunda started to mourn. Bitterly Peter thought, "There's no time even to mourn."

"We have to carry on," he insisted. They obeyed him, but now Jahunda was moaning in a low voice. Her tail burned with a fire-feeling that was more than she could bear. She no longer bothered to lift it but dragged it painfully along. There was Hedder up ahead, and a little beyond that, the pathway up the cliff.

"We're nearly there," Peter encouraged.

"Hedder, Hedder," Jahunda neighed. "We'll hide." And she began to lumber off in its direction.

"Yes, hide in Hedder," said Segui, trotting behind.

96

Smaller creatures were huddled in frightened groups outside, chattering and whimpering. They took no notice of Jahunda.

"Wrong! Wrong! Hedder is at sea level. It's not safe." Peter was frantic. But Jahunda had closed him off again; she didn't understand about the wave. Peter was now a captive on her back as she entered the cave mouth in total darkness.

At first Peter could see nothing, but the stench was appalling. Then he did see . . . red eyes at different levels, glaring. Suddenly creatures of every size rushed towards them and, with fearful roars and screeches, clamoured to kill.

Jahunda turned violently and galloped out, snorting. "They're all in there," she gasped. "The blind Tyrannosaurus and his mate. Others too. They've claimed it, are battling it out, fighting for possession. Come on! We'll follow the hadrosaurs up to the plain."

Jahunda was now in charge. Even Archelon heaved along behind. High on Jahunda's back, Peter felt completely powerless.

When he saw the path entrance right ahead and the animals hurry on by, Peter threw back his head and, with all the voice he had left, yelled, "Stop!"

There was such an urgency in his command that Jahunda stopped short and let him down. Then, undecided, with head bent low, she started to sway it again from side to side.

Peter turned to Segui, but he was too weak. He whimpered, "Water. Going back to lagoon. No water on the plain. Too hot." He came to Peter and nuzzled him. "Water," he pleaded. His breathing came out short and fast, his tongue hung limp, and there were dark blotches round his eyes. "Water; must."

Only then did Peter remember the waterfall.

"There *is* water – a waterfall. Up the path. Fresh water. It'll be good to drink."

"Good, good," Segui echoed. He went over to the pathway and listened. But the roaring of the creatures from the cave and the roaring from sea and wind deafened the waterfall. He turned away, disappointed.

"If you can't hear the water, smell it," Peter urged, remembering Jahunda telling him of their acute sense of smell.

Segui smelled, concentrating hard; but the air was filled with poisonous fumes. "No water," he said sadly, and turned away.

In desperation Peter went to Archelon. But he had retreated into his shell.

"There really *is* water up there, Archelon. We've got this far. Help me persuade them, please."

There was no response. Angrily Peter thumped on his shell. "We saved your life!" he cried. "Now save ours!"

Archelon came out of his shell and said, "I feel old now, and very dry. But I'll smell water anywhere if there is any to be had." He shifted and crawled over to the path. Lifting his beak he smelled. "Yes," he called back, not very convincingly. "Yes, I can smell water."

Then suddenly he stretched his head forward, gaped his mouth and nostrils wider, and for a second time smelled deep and long . . .

"Yes! There really *is* water up there," he barked excitedly. "Fresh water. Peter's right."

Eagerly, Archelon began to climb the path without waiting for the others. Segui turned back. He too went up the path a little way and drew in a long, deep breath which he held, tasting, feeling it. Then, "*Is* water!" he cried. "*Is*!" And he followed Archelon up the path.

"Come on, Jahunda, or we'll have to leave you."

Peter approached the swaying creature. It felt strange walking now; he could no longer feel anything, yet his legs were throbbing and throbbing.

"Don't go mad again, Jahunda," he pleaded; and, catching her head as it swung past, he hung on to it with all his might so that it stopped. Then he took the dinosaur face in his hands and saw in the eyes a vacancy more dangerous than he had ever experienced. He attempted to stare through the emptiness into the suffering behind. He stroked downwards between the eyes. He tried to reach deep into her mind, soothingly.

"Water, water. You are *so* thirsty and we're going to drink now. Come along."

Slowly, ever so slowly, he stroked and pulled her along, allowing her only to look straight ahead like a blinkered horse.

"Water," he whispered temptingly. "We're going to water."

Step by step they reached the entrance. Peter backed up it, encouraging her on to the narrow, enclosed path. After that she followed steadily, and Peter could turn to lead.

Chapter Sixteen

THE WATERFALL

Archelon scrabbled and tore at the path as he climbed, sweeping fallen branches aside in his effort to reach the water. Segui stumbled behind. The overhead branches tore afresh into his wound, and Peter, who was following, could hear his long, painful breathing; but he did not complain once. Behind Peter, Jahunda was silent, climbing as if in a dream.

Half-way up the path the feeling in Peter's legs came back; the sharp agonizing stabs made him pant with pain. Soon they were all exhausted, needing to rest. But Peter could just make out the time on his watch and he was sure that they had used up all the hours. He imagined the tidal wave, racing across the ocean at a great pace, pounding the coasts, swallowing everything in its path, and he knew they were still too low. Again he encouraged and hurried, and at last their efforts were rewarded by the sound of the waterfall gushing above them, drawing them on like a magnet.

Then they actually saw the waterfall a short way above, flowing as a pale tumbling sheet in the darkness from an outlet at the side of Woo-Kee cave. They drew extra energy from the sight, and were soon clambering on to the plateau next to Woo-Kee's dripping, fern-covered mouth.

"That's the cave where you're going to live," Peter shouted.

But the creatures' only thought was water. They stumbled towards it only to find the falls guarded. A threatening line of giant snails had slimed a thick, wide, ropy coil to stop intruders. It stretched across the plateau so that no one could get by.

"Climb on my back, Peter," Archelon instructed.

Gripping the rock with his scaly flippers, the turtle scraped a pathway through the slime. Segui and Jahunda squeezed the sticky stuff flat with the weight of their feet and approached the snails without difficulty. They were prepared to do battle with anything in order to drink. Once more it was Jahunda who surprised them with her sudden action.

"Bog-Brained gastropods away!" she cried, sweeping off two giant snails with her tail, making them slide on their own sheet of slime over the plateau edge to crush on the rocks below. But the agony was so great, she couldn't continue.

"Bog-Brained gastropods away!" Segui took over and, with a thwack, swept off the remaining three, one after the other.

They drank; slowly at first, then greedily, until at last they'd had enough. Peter's burning legs were cooled by the water and it helped stop the intense pain.

While their spirits slowly revived, Archelon and Peter rested on the plateau and watched as the two larger beasts climbed down on to the ridge and went right beneath the falls so that the great sheet of water rushed over their bodies, cooling them down. Peter wondered how much time they had left together. He turned to the sea turtle.

"Archelon, listen carefully. I came here to save you all from the wave. Your new home will be inside that cave. Will you be in charge of Segui and Jahunda? You'll have to make them stay inside for a long, long time. Outside, the wind and the sea will be poisoned. There will be darkness and dust in the sky, then stinging rains. And there may be great heat or great cold. Inside, you'll be safe. There's a deep pool where you can drink and swim. There are ferns and other things to eat. Stay until you find the outside safe to breathe. Go inside now, and I'll get the others to join you. I promise to come back one day soon to see how you are."

Archelon barked a farewell and trundled off into the cave.

It was while Segui and Jahunda were climbing towards him, with the brightness of the spray behind them, that Peter saw that the whole underneath of Jahunda's tail had been charred really black and that she could no longer hold it up. His eyes filled with tears. He hadn't thanked her yet for saving him.

"Jahunda, Jahunda . . ." he called, going towards her. But he was too late, for all at once there was a hollow roar, a high whistling – a noise so unearthly and terrible that it sounded like death trying to breathe. Almost immediately, a wind blew up; a sucking wind, that tried to pull them off the plateau and curl them in under the wave that was sweeping along. Every creature turned to see the tsunamis fill the horizon as it advanced, blacker than black and larger than the sky. It fed itself by pulling up in front of it a great wall of water hundreds of metres high. Fear strangled the onlookers' throats so they could not breathe.

After that everything happened suddenly but each second seemed to stretch in slow motion and last for ever.

Peter's voice was screaming, "To the cave. Into the cave."

Then he found he was grabbing for the disc in his pocket; but the bottom of its plastic case had melted and wouldn't open to allow him to get out the disc. He found he was sobbing as he smashed the case on a boulder until it split apart and he could hold the disc. Then he was pleading, "Take me home, take me home."

He saw the wave sweeping in through the gap in the mountains, heard the sizzling roar as it quenched the volcano's fire. Then it swallowed the lagoons, gulped up the beach and rolled in towards them.

Peter staggered towards the cave mouth, but never quite reached it. A huge snail slid out from behind a boulder, blowing from its mouth a carpet of foul-smelling foam, and headed straight for him.

Moments later, the roaring blackness came. It mounted higher and higher, curling in. Surely they wouldn't be high enough, couldn't be. The wave was far too large . . .

"Wait for me," he yelled, seeing Segui and Jahunda making for the cave mouth. But the snail was encircling Peter in a great coil of slime to prevent him from moving.

Filled with fury, Peter gripped the disc in his teeth, lunged at the snail, lifted it bodily, and was about to hurl it clear when everything went black.

Chapter Seventeen

THE BONFIRE

Peter landed back in the Palm House in Kew Gardens boiling hot all over and shaking like a leaf. His legs were throbbing unbearably from the burns. Worst of all, he still held the huge snail high, like a heavy trophy. Its horns were out and it was sliming a blanket of foam.

At the same time, Peter heard wailing and was just in time to catch sight of Elsie-Jane being carried out through the door by the other Peter Phillips.

This was followed by an almighty scream from the stout lady. Attracted by a glinting that came from Peter's disc – which he still clenched tightly in his teeth – she had seen the giant snail with all its foam. As she fell back in a dead faint, everyone gathered around.

"Elsie-Jane . . . I must get her back . . ."

Peter was about to launch himself after the other Peter Phillips when he changed his mind. "He can't see me with a giant snail – or the disc. He'll know where I've been and that I time-travelled instead of him. I'll be caught."

Peter stood, confused, clutching a snail which was desperately trying to escape, writhing its rubbery neck, poking him with its horns and slobbering all over him.

"I can't let a giant snail escape from the Cretaceous Age, especially not in Kew Gardens. That would *not* be a good idea. And supposing Ivan got to know that I had brought something back? Somehow I've got to get rid of it."

Another piercing shriek from outside told him that his mother had discovered Elsie-Jane being kidnapped. She had heard her baby wailing and looked up. After rescuing her she would be after him!

The people who weren't attending the stout lady rushed out to see what was happening. Taking this opportunity not to be seen, Peter made off as fast as his legs would allow through the door opposite. Trying to open it he bashed the snail, nearly dropping it. Outside, he stood, panicking.

What could he do with it? Whatever happened he couldn't let it drop: it would slime quickly away. Supposing it laid eggs? There would be giant snails everywhere in Kew. Then they'd spread throughout the country. No, somehow he would have to kill the foul thing.

Then he saw a thin plume of blue smoke rising over the hedge next to the Waterlily House and winding upwards through the trees.

"Of course! A bonfire! Just what I need!"

Quickly he made for the worm of smoke. The Waterlily House was being restored. It was now dry enough to tidy the mess and burn it after the recent rain. Peter went past a notice that said PRIVATE, and saw the bonfire, set back behind a hedge away from the public. He ran straight towards it and pitched himself into its centre.

The giant snail didn't like being pushed down into the heart of the blaze. It hissed and spat and spluttered, like a fizzling firework; then it began to cook.

The gardener, alerted by the peculiar noise, turned from wheeling his empty barrow. He saw his bonfire slowly being smothered by a fountain of foam, with this boy scrambling out. He couldn't believe his eyes.

"Hoy! You there! Hooligan! What on earth d'you think you're doing?"

The gardener grabbed his rake and charged at Peter, who made off round the Palm House towards the picnic blanket, with the gardener after him.

Peter was just in time to see the other Mr Phillips running off as fast as he could towards the main entrance. Ivan, whom he had been chasing, had completely disappeared.

Peter's mother was making her way back to the blanket, clutching the baby. She was hysterical.

"David, David, wake up! I had to rescue her all by myself. Where's Peter? That man said he found her! I tell you, he was the same man who was in our house the other day checking on Peter's computer! Oh! My baby! My baby! David, you must get the police."

Then she caught sight of Peter.

"Peter! There you are! What happened?"

Peter was a mass of scratches, burnt clothes, sulphurous hair, ashes and slime. But he realized that not only had he got rid of the huge snail, but also the bonfire had been a perfect disguise for his own appearance. Peter's father, who had slept through it all, was now awake. They both stared at him, horrified.

At first Peter was silent, searching for what to say. Then he came out with, "He was stealing our baby. He was stealing Elsie-Jane. So I rushed outside with her.

106

He grabbed Elsie-Jane, pushed me sideways into the bonfire and made off with her."

It certainly sounded good, and some of it was true. But now the gardener looked confused. He hadn't seen any baby – only foam.

Peter's appearance was enough to convince his father.

"You poor, brave boy! Are you hurt badly? Your hair's been completely burnt away! Your cap is ruined! Your legs are covered in ash!"

But Peter had sunk down suddenly on the rug. He fell back, unconscious with pain, next to his birthday cake. His father then discovered that the burns on his legs were really nasty under all the ash.

"The boy's much worse than we thought," he said, as he carried him to the car.

"He must be very fond of his new sister to have gone through all that," said Mrs Phillips, in tears, on the way to the hospital.

"He stinks – a real sulphur smell! As if he'd been inside a volcano," his father commented.

"Atchooo!" said Elsie-Jane.

"Are you quite sure these burns are only from a bonfire?" the doctor enquired. "They're very serious indeed. I'm afraid we shall have to keep him in."

Chapter Eighteen

PETER'S BIRTHDAY

Peter was in hospital for some time. During his fever, nightmare waves engulfed him. Chasms yawned, swallowing him into blazing fires; and he was so, so hot. He slipped from darkness into pitch black, remembering nothing; then he was struggling back towards the light.

When he eventually awoke, the nurse who had been sponging his brow said he'd called out in the middle of the night for someone called Jahunda and kept trying to thank her for saving him. Another time he'd sat bolt upright and asked everyone in the ward very loudly what baked snail in a bonfire would be like to eat.

Peter had his birthday in hospital. His parents brought him an extra parcel which by chance had arrived on the same day. It was from the Trustees of the Natural History Museum. Inside was a beautiful yellow pullover with two lines of cable down the front and back.

"It's not yours," his mother explained. "They couldn't find yours, but it's the right size and it *is* hand-knitted. Here, read the note."

We do hope this pullover will be an adequate substitute, as we are unable to find yours and it was not handed

in. This one has been unclaimed for a very long time.
We do hope it meets with your approval

With best wishes,
The Lost Property Department

Peter put it on.

"It suits you," his father pronounced.

At first Mrs Phillips looked suspiciously at the garment; then she had to agree that the standard of workmanship was just as fine as hers, and it did look good.

Peter suddenly remembered what had happened to his own jersey. "It's very nice of them," he said.

Ivan came to see him. He looked sullen and bitter. He thrust an envelope with a card at Peter. "I know it wasn't really your fault that your father came back at the last minute, but you knew I could still have got to the Palm House on my own in time to go with you. Kew's only a few miles away. I spent the whole day escaping from people. It wasn't fair. You promised . . ."

But when Peter apologized and then told Ivan that, as he was in hospital, Ivan would be in charge of all arrangements for the third journey, for them both, Ivan brightened up and soon became his usual self.

Peter propped himself against the pillows and described the second journey in great detail. It was important that Ivan knew as much as possible if he was to time-travel with him.

"I guessed your burns must be something to do with the Cretaceous Age, not just a bonfire in Kew," Ivan said. "Can I see your scars?"

He whistled in admiration when these were uncovered, but Peter began to feel tired at the sight of his own wounds, and soon wanted to sleep.

Later, Peter laughed at Ivan's card. It was a drawing of a huge egg, designed on his computer. Inside it said:

Did you know that it takes $4\frac{1}{2}$ hours to boil an Ostrich Egg?

Two days later, Ivan came round with plans for the third journey fully completed. He was almost carried away by his own efficiency.

"I've found a special Easter Week excursion that goes to Cheddar Gorge and Wookey Hole on the twenty-fifth. It leaves Victoria Coach Station at nine o'clock. First we have to see the Cheddar Gorge, but lunch is outside Wookey Hole at one thirty, before visiting the caves. It's perfect. Then we gather outside Wookey Hole at four fifteen to come back. I've booked two tickets and my father's paying. Yours is for your birthday present. I said it was vital that we made a map of the Jurassic and Cretaceous rock of the area for next term at school. I didn't tell him we'd finished that project, but he'll never know. Anyway, he said we were quite old enough to go there together. He even said it would be good for me to make an expedition like that."

"Thanks, Ivan. That's brilliant." Peter smiled.

The day before Peter went home, his mother came, bringing good news.

"It's all very exciting, Peter. Our new fern – or rather very old fern, as we now have to call it – has been collected and taken to Kew. It's a unique cycad tree fern and is going to be named *Cycas phillipsii*. It only had a fossil number before. And the whole Phillips family is invited to an evening banquet at the Savoy Hotel, where, at a special ceremony attended by fern experts from all over the world, we are to be presented with a trophy! It's the evening of April the twenty-fifth at eight fifteen. That's Daddy's last day with us before returning to Singapore, so it's worked out well."

Peter's face fell. "But Ivan and I are going to Wookey Hole that day. I can't come with you."

He knew there wouldn't be any point to his life ever again if he didn't go back to see if Archelon, Jahunda and Segui had survived. He'd promised, and he would keep his word. All he remembered before he left them was a roaring blackness. Did that mean the wave *had* drowned them?

But his mother was smiling. "Don't worry, everything's been sorted out by Ivan and me. Your coach arrives back at seven thirty. You're to get a taxi straight to the Savoy. After the banquet, the Phillips family has been invited to stay overnight as guests of the Horticultural Society. Ivan can stay, and he'll share a room with you. It couldn't have worked out better."

The following day, Peter went home. Ivan brought round an Ordnance Survey map so they could check exactly where to stand to time-travel. "They tell us on the disc, don't they?"

Peter put the disc in his computer, and found that a detail from the Ordnance Survey map of the area was given, with the point of departure magnified to show them the precise spot to be. Using the grid reference, they were able to mark off the same place on their own map.

"It's a bit strange the grid reference isn't at Wookey Hole itself, but further up the hill slope. Look, it's in this nature reserve, near a place called Ebbor Gorge."

111

"Wait a bit . . . Wookey Hole may go back that far *under* the ground."

"We'd better stay above ground, though. Don't forget that sixty-five millions years have passed. The land would have changed."

"Yes, Hedder Cave – which the tsunamis must have flooded – probably got eroded. There isn't a Hedder or Cheddar Cave today, only a Cheddar Gorge, and that's a mile or two from Wookey."

"Maybe everything will be different. You said a whole year had gone by on your second journey. It will just depend where the time loops touch from our time zone to theirs for the third one."

The evening before they left, Peter and Ivan followed their usual routine. They plugged the Energy Activator Power Pack into Ivan's computer and locked his door securely.

Chapter Nineteen

THE THIRD JOURNEY

The coach party had already visited the Cheddar Gorge.
Now everyone was at Wookey Hole, eating sandwiches
in the picnic places or inside the self-service restaurant
– everyone except the two boys, who had slipped away
to find the spot they'd marked with a red cross on
their map.

"Let's follow this footpath that starts above Wookey
Hole and leads up to the nature reserve," Peter sug-
gested. "We've got plenty of time; and it's not as obvious
as going by road – if anyone is following."

At first all went well. The countryside was beautiful:
it felt very ancient and unchanged over hundreds of
years. Their path was edged with primroses, celandines
and violets, and to one side a small stream (the River
Axe, they noted) rushed and tumbled over a stony bed.
They changed to a more direct track, a higher path, that
led up over the fields. The contours were very close
together on the map and Ivan found that he was soon
out of breath as he climbed. The suitcase he carried
caused most of the trouble, and its heaviness – for someone only on a one-day outing – had caused a certain
amount of merriment on the coach.

"Going to emigrate?"

"Bringing your own sandwiches are you?" they had laughed.

But after the embarrassment in Kew Gardens, Ivan had packed his rope and equipment carefully. This time they wouldn't be seen.

"Leave the case behind, Ivan," Peter said, exasperated.

"No, I want to bring back specimens and I want to be able to defend myself with a bit more than a penknife."

"It doesn't *work*, Ivan, bringing things back. It only causes trouble."

"You didn't bring back trouble when you got your fern, did you?"

Peter realized Ivan had guessed where the fern had come from. He was silent.

They reached the top of a high field and climbed over a stile leading into a wood. Ahead was a craggy limestone gorge sprouting bunches of fern and trailings of ivy. Now they needed to turn left to reach a footbridge which crossed the stream. To do this they had to scramble down the gorge a little way and climb again once the bridge was crossed. At the bottom, Ivan needed to rest; so they sat by the stream to eat their sandwiches and drink their tins of Coke. There was still a while before 2.30 p.m., with everything going to plan – until it began to rain.

At first it was a spring shower; then it turned into a downpour. They started to squelch up the footpath, which had changed into a sea of sticky mud that clung to their shoes until it felt as if they were carrying half the hillside on the end of their feet. It took ages to climb, and now suddenly they had less time to get there.

Eventually Ivan spotted their destination through the driving rain – a small craggy outcrop with a flat summit, just off the path to the left. On the rain-soaked map they saw they had only to climb this and they would reach the right place.

"Come on! It's almost two thirty."

Ivan forgot the weight of his suitcase in his excitement. He left the path and plunged through the ivy and ferns and began to climb the crag, dragging his suitcase with one hand and clutching on to ivy roots with the other. Peter – just to be on the safe side – got the disc out of his pocket and held it ready as he followed. Ivan had neared the top; he flung his suitcase up ahead of him on to the summit and hauled himself up. Peter followed – only to see waiting for them the other Mr Phillips, glowering down through the slanting rain.

Ivan grabbed his suitcase, ready to hurl it at the man.

"Wait, wait!" shouted Mr Phillips urgently. "I'm only here to warn you, you mustn't take that suitcase to the Cretaceous Age. You're not allowed to bring things back from the past. It upsets the balance of things."

"*You* seem to have equipment with you," Ivan retorted.

"That's just scientific equipment – to measure – to take photos. It's not for bringing things back. Also, it's far too dangerous for small boys like you to travel back without protection. Let me at least go with you. We could all three travel together."

With only seconds to go before 2.30 p.m., there was no time to argue; so both Ivan and Mr Phillips leaned forward to grasp the disc. But because Ivan was still clutching his heavy suitcase and Mr Phillips his scientific equipment, they had no free hands to steady themselves. Slipping on the mud, they both slid, falling heavily against a boulder, dislodging it so that it, too, slid on the sticky mud to reveal a dark hole beneath. Out of this spilled some musty-smelling air. Into it shot the shiny disc. Peter clawed frantically at the boulder for balance, but found he was sliding too, then falling to follow the disc down into the round, dark hole. There was a crunch as he landed; then silence.

Chapter Twenty

WOO-KEE

"We've killed him!" Ivan yelled.

He turned on Mr Phillips. "And you caused all this to happen, Bog-Brain! Quick! Get my torch from the suitcase!"

But Mr Phillips stood there, cleaning the rain off his pebbly spectacles, waiting the eight seconds he knew it would take for the boy to return from the Cretaceous Age. The downpour, too, stopped suddenly, and the sun came out, shining as if nothing had happened.

Ivan dragged the suitcase over to the hole himself, wrenched it open, got out his torch and shone it down into the blackness. He could just make out the form of Peter, lying horribly still on top of what looked like a pile of old bones. As he watched, the body began to come to, heaving in short gasps, trying to breathe.

"He's alive! He's making a weird noise!"

Mr Phillips gaped. The boy must have come back down there. Or did he really fall and not time-travel at all? He hurried over, and listened above the hole.

"Thank goodness! It sounds as if he's not dead, only winded. My God, there's no air down there for him to breathe! Perhaps he did time-travel but came back down there and just can't breathe because there's no air . . . It smells like a million years old. We'll have to get him out fast."

Suddenly Mr Phillips jumped into action. "That rope there, in your suitcase . . . If I tie it to a tree, you could let yourself down and loop it around him. I'll pull you up one at a time."

Ivan glared. "Hurry, then, if you're going to help."

Soon, Ivan was being lowered into the cave on the end of a rope. He still didn't trust Mr Phillips one little bit. "All he wants is that disc, so he's not going to get it – not until we're *both* safely up."

The cave was huge, airless and strangely dry, and as Ivan neared the ground, he shone the torch below him. Through the gloom he saw immediately that Peter was lying on top of what were undoubtedly the skeletons of two enormous dinosaurs. "Oh, no! The disc has brought them back – but it's killed them!"

There they were, lying side by side . . . in a dip in the ground where a pool might once have been. Peter had crashed right through one of their rib-cages when he landed: the rib-cage must have saved his life.

Ivan swung himself to the side as he neared the ground; then he untied the rope and climbed through the bones to reach Peter. He was trying to breathe in gasps that echoed eerily round the cave. Even by torchlight, his face had gone a funny blue.

Ivan propped the torch on one of the dinosaur's shoulder-blades. He knew he had to work fast; there was no time to be afraid. He hitched a loop of rope round Peter's body, lashed it round once more under the arms and then shouted, "OK. Up!"

Very slowly Peter's body ascended and for a moment blocked the hole. Only then did Ivan feel suddenly alone and scared. He shone the torch around. It was so black that the beam seemed no more than a single star shining in a starless night. He looked for other exits from the chamber, but there were none: the cave was perfectly sealed.

"I've got him up! Now you!" the voice echoed from above, as the rope dropped quickly down.

Ivan looked for the disc and found it glinting among the bones. He stuffed it inside his sock, then arranged the rope under his arms.

"I've got the disc! I'm ready! You can haul me up now!"

The ascent was painfully slow. Ivan kept spinning round and round. Suddenly the pulling stopped and he hung in mid-air, like a spider on the end of a thread. Then he was really frightened. The hole in the roof seemed very small and far away, and he was getting exhausted because there was no more air left to breathe. He began to choke. He knew he wouldn't make it, would be stifled on the end of the rope and brought up dead.

But Mr Phillips was only catching his breath – he wasn't used to such exertion. He continued to pull hard, and soon Ivan was hauled into the light, gasping. For a few moments he couldn't see, and he knew that Mr Phillips would be hunting for the disc on his body. But when he could see, Mr Phillips was over beside Peter, making sure he was recovering.

"Don't move him," he instructed, still panting, as Ivan came over. "Let him get his breath back gradually. Stay with him. My car's parked higher up the gorge, not too far away. I'll get a blanket and Thermos of hot tea. Then we'll help him to the car together."

He raced off, leaving Ivan feeling very ashamed. He hadn't even asked for the disc.

As Peter began to recover, Ivan asked him what he remembered of the eight seconds.

"Nothing. Nothing at all. I remember falling but everything went black, just like when the tsunamis came."

Ivan told him what had happened to them, and about the rescue. But as he explained, Peter took the torch and staggered over to the hole. After peering down for a while, he was sobbing and trying to speak at the same time.

"Just look down there, Ivan, I've brought the dinosaurs back and I've killed them. I didn't mean to . . . The disc must have fallen right between them and brought them back. They must have been recalled by it after the eight seconds . . . Both would have come back if they were touching. I said they wouldn't survive a journey back to modern time, and I was right – and so was Mr Phillips. He *did* try to warn us . . .'

Ivan tried to comfort Peter, but he was distraught.

"If . . . if they were recalled and there was no air in the cave, then they would have suffocated almost at once. Maybe they aged suddenly sixty-five million years and their bodies disintegrated into dust – like when they open a mummies' tomb."

"Listen, Peter," Ivan said gently. 'One of the dinosaur skeletons saved your life. You fell right on to its rib-cage, and, as it shattered, it broke your fall."

Peter looked up at Ivan, then gradually stopped sobbing, exhausted with grief. "You *all* rescued me – you, Mr Phillips and the dinosaurs. Thank you. You must have been scared Ivan, going down. And I was so rude about your suitcase. If you hadn't brought all that equipment—"

"Listen, it's all right. I wasn't too afraid – not to begin with anyway. It was terribly exciting sliding down into the cave and seeing the two skeletons in that enormous cavern. It really is vast down there – huge. No one – no human that is – has ever been inside it before . . ."

"I have."

"Oh yes, I forgot. You were inside it sixty-five million years ago, when it was Woo-Kee."

"Yes," thought Peter. "In fact I must have fallen through that hole in the roof where the sun used to filter in through the ferns."

This only made Peter burst into further tears. "But, I . . . I . . . took so long trying to rescue them from the wave. And it was all useless, useless saving them. I meant to go back and thank them, see whether they'd survived. Instead . . . now look what I've done!"

When Mr Phillips returned he was pleased to see the boy recovered – but couldn't understand why he was over by the hole, sobbing.

When Peter saw Mr Phillips he said, "Thank you for saving me. Ivan, give him back his disc. I . . . I never want to see it again, or the dinosaur bones. I want to go home now."

Reluctantly, Ivan gave Peter's disc to Mr Phillips, who said, "Dinosaur bones? What dinosaur bones?"

"Yes, I didn't tell you. It was the dinosaur bones down there that saved Peter. They broke his fall."

Mr Phillips was staggered. He leaned right over the hole and, with the torch, tried to identify the shapes in the pile of bones. "Good grief!" he gasped. "They're fantastic!" He flung the torch aside. "I'll take some properly lit photos of the bones – and then we must seal the hole at once in case the skeletons crumble further in the air."

While Mr Phillips was excitedly taking photos, Ivan poured Peter a mug of tea and had some himself. Then Mr Phillips and Ivan tried to push the boulder back over the hole, but it was too heavy. Ivan discovered that his suitcase fitted the hole perfectly, so they packed it tight with mud and stones until no more air could get inside.

Peter had gone very quiet, and Ivan was worried. Peter refused Mr Phillips's kind offer to take them back to London by car. He knew Mr Phillips would talk non-stop about what he, as a scientist, thought of as a wonderful "find" of dinosaur bones, whereas they knew them as Jahunda and Segui. So Mr Phillips drove the boys back to their coach, reaching it at 4.25 p.m., just in the nick of time for the departure.

Chapter Twenty-one

THE FERN TROPHY

When they arrived by taxi at the Savoy Hotel, Peter and Ivan were plunged immediately into huge, hot, foaming bubble baths. Peter had suffered on the coach journey back. His body was bruised and aching from the fall. The bath was exactly what he needed to get him through the evening.

The poshness of everything in the Savoy was like being in a dream. Fresh clothes had been laid out for them on their beds, and when they were dressed they were called down into the banqueting room where they had a sumptuous meal with a large glass of champagne. Then the speeches and ceremony began. It was all very important and formal.

"We are here today to honour the Phillips family for their work in the preservation of a unique plant. Because of this family's care and attention, a new, but very ancient, fern tree has been saved for posterity. Experts throughout the world have delighted in the discovery of a Cycad thought to have been extinct for sixty-five million years being found at the end of a row of cabbages in a suburb of London. Scientists are of the opinion that the fern seed must have come from outer space, carried in on a speck of dust – commonly known as a shooting star."

"How lovely to think that a shooting star landed in my garden." Mrs Phillips's eyes twinkled. "And to land so accurately like that – right on the end of my row of cabbages, so it could be watered!"

"Sshh darling!" said Mr Phillips.

"Cycad fern trees, as we all know, grow very slowly indeed. The oldest pot plant in the world is a Cycad fern tree in our own famous Palm House. However, *Cycas phillipsii* seems to be growing in a time zone all of its own and has already started to produce a seed-cone. We'll be able to send seeds to Wakefield Place. Australia needs a few, and New Zealand wants to establish *Cycas phillipsii* in its fern collection."

Peter wondered whether the glade the fern had come from had been drowned beneath the wave, in which case he really had saved it. He felt only half awake as the speeches came to an end, and hardly noticed when his mother went up to receive the trophy until the clapping broke out. She looked radiant as she stepped down from the dais, and as she came towards them she beamed with pride. Peter turned to look at Elsie-Jane in her travel-cot, but she had slept peacefully throughout the whole event.

Later, Peter and Ivan slept in their own suite in wonderfully comfortable beds. The following morning, Mr Phillips prepared to go to the airport to fly back to Singapore. He had a choice of six free newspapers to read at breakfast. The headlines on most of these declared dramatically MAGNIFICENT DINOSAUR FIND

The exciting discovery of two dinosaurs of the type

Opisthocoelicaudia in a newly found ancient cavern above the far end of the Wookey Hole cave system by two boys, Ivan Topolski and Peter Phillips of Richmond, Surrey, while on an Easter Holiday coach expedition, has astounded the whole world. These giant late sauropods, of the kind known to most children as Brontosaurus or Apatosaurus, are a staggering find. They are the first of this type from the Late Cretaceous Age ever to be discovered in the British Isles. With skeletons almost perfectly intact, they make the finest complete specimens in Europe. The two adult dinosaur skeletons are being taken very carefully in sealed, airtight containers to the Natural History Museum, where they are to be preserved with a new special gel prior to being inspected and drawn by the Department of Palaeontology.

"Good gracious!" he called out. "That is my son!"

Everyone turned from their breakfasts, some spilling their tea.

The articles were accompanied by a series of dark and interesting photographs, taken by Mr Peter Phillips (no relation).

The two boys were immediately famous. They read every article. Ivan was amazed that the other Mr Phillips had taken so little credit for himself. Peter puzzled over the word 'adult' in the article. Two adult dinosaurs, it said. Perhaps he'd been wrong? Perhaps they weren't Segui and Jahunda, but two other fully grown dinosaurs he had killed?

When they went back to school, both Ivan and Peter were embarrassed by new admirers wanting to know about their dinosaur find. Although Peter's family winning a fern trophy at the Savoy Hotel was a special event mentioned in assembly, it was the dinosaurs that captured everyone's imagination. The two boys were celebrated by press and public alike.

Peter rather enjoyed his glamorous existence at school. Now he was so certain that the two adult dinosaurs he had killed were ones he'd never met, it didn't matter so much.

But at home, Peter was often moody and silent. So many questions about his dinosaurs remained mysteries, and his chance to return to see whether they had survived had been wasted. He mostly went out jogging or played for hours with Elsie-Jane.

"What are you doing, dear, staring into the baby's eyes like that?" asked his mother.

"I'm teaching her think-speaking," he answered.

Mrs Phillips shrugged. All that publicity was going to her son's head.

Chapter Twenty-two

THE EXPLANATION

Peter and Ivan donated their dinosaur skeletons to the Natural History Museum. Their marvellous gifts were to remain on view in the new Dinosaur Gallery for several weeks so that the public could get a chance to see them before further research was carried out. Both families had been invited to a reception – a kind of Private View – attended by top palaeontologists. At this occasion the boys were to receive an award of their own choice, as well as being given free entry to the museum for them and their families for life.

When the day arrived, both the Phillips and Topolski families journeyed to Kensington in cars hired specially for them. Peter went straight over to stare down at the two skeletons. They had been carefully laid out, enclosed inside an enormous air-sealed cabinet. Soon his heart was beating away.

The palaeontologist in charge, seeing Peter staring, came over.

"Yes, it is rather strange, isn't it? The larger dinosaur, at one stage in its life, had all the bones on the underneath of its tail charred black. It must have narrowly escaped some disastrous fire."

To his surprise, the palaeontologist saw several tears trickle down the boy's face. He was touched; this was obviously a sensitive child.

But Peter said, "Jahunda! Then it *was* you all the time."

"And there's another interesting thing," the scientist continued. "We believe that the slightly younger male might even have suffered a limp – probably caused by a shoulder injury inflicted during his youth. Can you see . . . over there . . . how the shoulder-blade bone was damaged at one point, but then healed over?"

Peter knew exactly where to look. "Segui! You *have* to be Segui!"

"They're really both in a remarkable state of preservation. They seem to have had a very varied diet, too. We found all sorts of things from analysing the area where their stomachs had been."

Peter said aloud, "But I don't understand. How old do you think they both were when they died?"

"Oh, both fully grown – although we haven't been able to find out their exact ages yet. We've done a carbon-dating, but something's gone slightly wrong. They can only make them out to be several hundred years old – when they're more likely to be around sixty-five million years old . . . They both certainly lived a full, long life in their time, though – despite their handicaps of the limp and the burns. It's all very exciting. And the female reached a good old age – probably something like two hundred years."

Peter rushed over to grab Ivan. "It's them! It *is* them, after all!"

The two boys wandered round and round the case

looking intently at every part of the skeletons.

"That means they did survive the wave. I was able to save them so they could live a full life."

The two boys were jubilant. "Ha! We did it!" And they slapped palms together.

Mrs Phillips noticed their pleasure and felt suddenly very relieved. Peter was looking his old self again. Everything would be all right.

Ivan was already trying to work things out. "So, what must have happened is this: the disc must have gone on its own to the Cretaceous Age and brought back the two skeletons, which were already dead in the cave – and may have been dead there for hundreds of years already, for all we know. That is why they are in such good condition, don't you see? Instead of being sixty-five million years old, they may only have been dead for a few hundred years before the disc brought them back. Jahunda may have gone back to the cave when she knew she was going to die. Maybe Segui went there to die much later, when he was old."

"And they must have been able to survive after they left the cave, when conditions got better. The palaeontologist said they seemed to have had a very varied diet."

For a while they were silent, taking in everything that must have happened. Then Peter looked wistful. "I was still never able to thank Jahunda for saving my life, though, and I never really said goodbye to them properly."

"Yes, but you did save them, Peter, for then . . . for now . . . for us . . . for everyone."

. The presentation ceremony had begun. After the formal speeches – which included profuse votes of thanks from the Natural History Museum to the two boys – each was presented with his special award, at which everyone burst into laughter when they saw what the boys had chosen. They were presented with a dinosaur coprolite each, on a silver plate inscribed with the details of their find. Ivan was overwhelmed. He had wanted one of these more than anything, and Peter was pleased that he had chosen the same thing for himself.

But the clapping and whistling were interrupted by a shriek from Mrs Phillips: "That's him! That's him again!" Mrs Phillips pointed an accusing finger at a man who was beaming at Ivan and Peter from beside the case of the giant three-toed sloth. "There's that man! The one who tried to steal my baby! The one who came to check on Peter's computer!" And she flung herself protectively over her baby's cot.

Elsie-Jane was furious. She screamed with annoyance. Up to now, she had been really enjoying the occasion.

"Oh, no! How embarrassing!" said Ivan, going over to pacify Mr Phillips, while Peter went over to pacify his mother.

Things were calmed down by the arrival of the champagne, and the little upset was quickly forgotten. Ivan was soon engrossed in talking to a sandy-haired man, while drinking champagne with one hand and clutching his coprolite fiercely with the other. Before long, he brought him to meet Peter. The tall, lanky man held out a long-fingered hand for Peter to shake. He looked kindly and rather interesting.

"At last I've managed to meet you, Peter Phillips," he said. "I'm Mr Witkins. I've only just managed to get here – my plane was delayed. I've got something to return to you that's yours."

To Peter's surprise, Mr Witkins took out the disc and pressed it into his hand.

"But I d-don't understand," Peter stuttered.

"You see, it's very simple ... It doesn't work for anyone else. I'm the person who invented the disc. I ought to know."

Ivan butted in. "So you mean I wouldn't have been able to travel back with Peter on *any* of the three journeys?"

"I'm afraid not. The disc will bring things back from bygone ages, and also return things that come from there, but only Peter can travel from our age."

"Then why did Mr Phillips try so hard to get it back, if he couldn't use it? It doesn't make sense," said Peter.

"Because he didn't *know* he couldn't use it," explained Mr Witkins. "You see, for security reasons, I had been told to impregnate the disc with a chemical that read your thumb and fingerprints and sealed them in when you first withdrew the disc from its cellophane film."

"I did smell a chemical smell, I remember now."

"Well, from that moment on, the disc would only respond to your grasp; it's locked inside the disc for ever. No one else in the world can use it to travel with, not even me."

"So that's why the other Mr Phillips gave it back."

"You must understand how frustrated and disappointed one of our top scientists must have felt, to make him chase you the way he did. He was also trying to warn you not to bring things back; because one is only

131

allowed to time-travel, so to speak, if one accepts the moral code not to upset the balance of things."

Ivan blushed and looked guilty, until Peter squeezed his hand. "If you hadn't put that rope in your suitcase, I would have died," he whispered.

"Your disc is the first experiment of its kind to have been made," Mr Witkins continued. "And so expensive to create that it has to be one of the most valuable objects in the whole world. Developing a second disc – Series Two, Experiment Two – using other time loops for other journeys, will take years, as you can imagine, and a further enormous outlay of money from both the United States Government and the Canadian Government. So you see, Peter, you've become rather important to us. Nobody can use the rest of the time travel journeys we have devised on your disc except for you. And I've been talking to your friend, Ivan, here, and he has told me all about your remarkable power of think-speaking, as you call it. You have a rare gift indeed, and are probably exactly the right kind of person we needed to go on these journeys anyway.

"Now, because of the courage and understanding you have already shown on *this* journey, we hope to find out from you whether our meteorite prediction was correct. We will need to do a kind of debriefing on your dinosaur time travel, if that is OK with you?"

"Of course, I'll tell you everything that happened."

"And I think perhaps we ought to explain a few things to your Mother . . ." Mr Witkins looked over to where poor Mrs Phillips was standing, still rather bemused.

"Yes, there are a lot of mysteries she would like

explained – like why my burns and bruises were so bad."

"And what really happened to your yellow jersey and sandwich box," added Ivan.

"Well, I did *tell* her that they'd been eaten by a dinosaur . . ."

Rose Tremain
Journey to the Volcano £2.99

'Fear was racing in all their hearts, fear for everyone and everything they loved, fear for what seemed like the end of the world.'

George's world had been transformed. His sudden removal from his father and home in London to his mother's Sicilian family on the remote slopes of Mount Etna hurls him into a dangerous and wonderful summer: strange rituals, a sinister sense of the past and a vibrant vision of the present: then, an angry volcano threatens his whole existence . . .

Rose Tremain: 'She is among the most prolific and experienced of the twenty "Best of Young British Novelists" . . . and certainly one of the most gifted' MAIL ON SUNDAY

Geoffrey Trease
The Popinjay Mystery £3.50

Charles II holds court in London and Sam Pepys holds the key to Britain's sea defences at the Navy office. Both men are surrounded by political corruption and intrigue.

When young Lieutenant Denzil Swift rides to help rescue Pepys and his companions from Highwaymen, he finds himself at the centre of a desperate plot which threatens the fragile stability of the realm.

This fast-paced adventure reaches a thrilling climax in a river chase on the Thames at high tide, midnight.